THREE RIMS

AND A

HUBCAP

THREE RIMS
AND A
HUBCAP

The Mafia Ministry as Night Falls . . .

Gentile

Library of Congress Control Number:		2016904935
ISBN:	Hardcover	978-1-5144-7921-6
	Softcover	978-1-5144-7920-9
	eBook	978-1-5144-7919-3

Print information available on the last page.

Rev. date: 03/28/2016

To order additional copies of this book, contact:
Xlibris
1-888-795-4274
www.Xlibris.com
Orders@Xlibris.com
734393

*The full impact of any issue
can only be measured by the one bearing its weight.*

– Gentile

Dedication

The recent passing of my dad and brother still pains me beyond anything I have ever experienced. It is particularly difficult because my dad has read most of this manuscript and was extremely eager for me to publish it. He said, "This book has certainly captured the zeitgeist of the era, and if I didn't know better, I would believe you lived during this period of extreme poverty, segregation, share cropping, and church ideology."

My brother, Jewel, brought many ideas to the production of this work simply by being Jewel. He truly lived a life full of joy and satirical wit, and he enjoyed being with his friends and family. It was never too early or too late for him to enjoy himself and pull stunts with all of us so he could laugh. If you knew him, reading this book will surely reveal much of his unique brilliance and personality. So to my great dad, Jesse Everett, and my loving brother, Jewel Everett, I dedicate this book. Without you both guiding and protecting me my entire life, this book could not have been written. I love you, Reb (Dad). I love you, Jewel. And since I'm the only man left in our immediate family, I'll do my best to represent the principles of God and do what is wise because I know it's what you both would have wanted.

I love you guys forever, and thanks for the guidance and the priceless contributions you made in my life.

Agape,
Gentile

TO THE READER

THIS IS A work of fiction. It was written merely for entertainment purposes. It does, however, point to the idea that all who are involved in ministry have personal challenges that must be dealt with while positively making an impact in kingdom building. So the author, using a fertile imagination, constructed this interesting story for the purpose of understanding the possibilities that could result in ministry leadership. Please be advised that this author does not accept or condone moral failure, and the engagements of kingdom building should reflect the purity for which it represents. This is recreational reading for those who seek entertainment in their spiritual plight. It is suggested that you read it for laughter and intrigue and enjoy the characters that emerge in this unfolding saga.

IT WAS HOT and sticky down in the Mississippi Delta in mid-August 1942 when young Dominique Washington was introduced to a life that appeared to have been reserved just for her. By now, at the age of only eighteen, her beauty was already budding into what anyone would call model fine. She was slim with very smooth brown skin, long flowing hair accentuated her slender face, and her smile was as bright as the morning sun. Her teeth were so perfectly even and appeared freshly polished with each grin. She was even blessed with shapely bow legs, and when she worked it, it was as if the motion and rhythm of poetry were her vehicle of transportation. Eighteen was her age, but twenty-one was her look. Her greatest desire was to be a lady. But not just an ordinary lady, but a lady of distinction, grace, and class because in her mind, you were not a lady without the most opulent surroundings and without enjoying all the best in clothes, foods, and living in general. Her idea about herself could not be explained because in 1942, blacks in the South were struggling to survive.

Although she was acutely aware of this reality, she never accepted it as her way of life. In school, other young girls were always trying to fight with her because so many were very jealous of the attention given to her at this very early age. She was a diva dime, for sure. She learned quickly to stay away from many of her peers because the threats of fights, she fancied, would undermine her thirst for great beauty. Although born poor, she believed that her place in life was to be in bright lights and before an audience where all eyes were affixed on her.

She loved attention and money and was glad to receive either. When school ended in the summer of 1942, she asked her mother if she could go to work with her, knowing her mother, Ms. Louise Washington, was a domestic worker in the home of retired colonel Jefferson Johnson and Mrs. Ellie Johnson. Young Dominique believed if she were with her mother, the haters in their "hood" would forget about her and not bother her because her mother would be there to provide protection for her. So Dominique asked her mother, Ms. Louise, if she could go with her to work and promised she would not get in the way and would do only what she was told to do.

Her mother said, "Yes, darling, I think that'll be just fine. Besides, the colonel is having a little dinner party 'dissennin,' and maybe you could help out with serving the white folks and such as that." So Dominique wore some of her usual clothes and packed a nice outfit for the party. It had been some time since Colonel and Mrs. Ellie had seen young Dominique, and they were very astonished at how beautiful she had become. And after she dressed for the elegant affair, her charm and beauty were raised to another level. The women and men couldn't seem to take their eyes off this vision of loveliness. And once the men were separated from the women, one of the southern gentlemen waved to the colonel and said, "When do you plan to break her in to the special duties befitting her? Now if you are not planning to let me know because I could easily have a special place for a cute niggra girl like her, I thought to ask you first, seeing she was from the pile of property you already own in her ma, Ms. Louise."

The colonel replied, "Well, I been thinking about that every since I saw her today, and Louise is still going strong in that department. She's only thirty-five now and has plenty more miles left in her engine. She roars loud and steady for me."

The colonel continued, "I think I'll start marinating young Dominique, and in a few weeks, I'll start helping her to develop a craving for a little flesh pole, you know, start teaching her the basic things about pleasing the boss. If she is anything like her mother, she'll have the whole thing licked after just a few sessions." The colonel's special guest, Mr. Georgie Asbury, said, "Colonel, you have a gift at breaking in pretty niggra girls like nobody I have ever seen, and I believe this one is the most beautiful one yet. Man, take her out of school around sixteen and you'll have a pot to plant many seeds in probably for the rest of your seed planting days. Besides, at her age, man, she'll still be in her soil prime when young Jeff becomes a man. And if y'all take care of her and what you leave behind, your son Jeff can finish planting in her pot until she's too ripe to press up against anymore."

The colonel replied, "Well, I hadn't considered that before, but I'll certainly take that into account now." As the dinner party continued, the level of the colonel's desire was raised to enlist young Dominique into the process of pleasure abuse, and he seemed to ponder his next move in smoothly molding and directing her to fit in his lewd scheme. Within the next few weeks of this hot, steamy summer, he encouraged Louise to bring her daughter to work every day behind the guise of some possible summer employment. After all, she was out school, and he sold this idea to her mother that more money could be made for the family if Dominique became part of his house, his employment pool. Louise agreed and proceeded to follow the colonel's suggestion.

But what the colonel was not aware of was the many facets to Louise's life. Louise was an extremely clever young woman in the art of deception. She was a leader in the local church and had made an influential reputation in ministry through the church's music ministry. She was truly endowed with the gift of singing, and much demand was made upon her talent to perform at funerals, revivals, weddings, and their weekly worship services. Each time she presented herself in a soloistic posture, the congregants would offer their highest attention because they knew her incredible voice would reverberate throughout the building. They had grown accustomed to her jazzy slurs, chromatic runs, and staccatos that would add greater pleasure to the songs she performed. She would routinely excite and evoke great emotional responses from the members.

Talented as she was, many wondered why she didn't pursue professional singing. It was later thought that her loyalty to the colonel and accepting his words as gospel had greater weight than anything else. It was believed that she could not tear herself away from him because she was not a slave in the legal sense, but the colonel was successful in convincing her that he was her boss and that could never be challenged, and trust me, it was never challenged or questioned.

Yes, she loved singing and working in her local church, but her love for the church and her loyalty to the colonel did not come close to fulfilling her financial requirements for the services she was rendering. She would attend church services regularly, and at the altar call, when congregants would gather for prayer, Sister Louise had one thing on her mind, and that was for the Lord to shower her with more, more, and more money.

After a few years of employing this practice, no more money seemed to rain down. The family's needs continued to escalate with the rising costs for goods and services. With the rising cost of living, Sister Louise felt desperate. Then a moment of revelation appeared in the next week's worship service. Sister Louise heard a guest minister from Maryland named the Reverend J. W. Wilson, who preached from the text which addressed, "Seek and Ye Shall Find." And without any theological foundation with which to appropriately frame an accurate interpretation, she immediately framed the passage into her personal system of materialistic desire and decided it was God's will that she live better and enjoy more of the good life. So she left church and immediately designed and implemented a more complex scheme to make more money by crossing the lines of the law while maintaining her pristine reputation within her community and among her fellow church members.

As night falls . . .

That night, she called to her home a special cousin named Solomon Patterson, affectionately known as Skeeter because of his reputation with the ladies. He believed in carousing with many, and when possible, entertaining multiple ladies at the same time. Louise and Skeeter shared a very special relationship. They were kids of sisters and grew up as brother and sister. Also, they had a special bond of love for each other and would protect each other at all cost. Even as children, they would lie to cover infractions and acts of disobedience each of them would commit. Wow! Anytime Louise called, Skeeter would drop everything to attend to his cousin's needs. So when Skeeter arrived at Louise's place, he said, "What's shaking, cuz? Let's make this happen quick becuz I have these hot ones in the car, and they all waitin' on Big Daddy Skeeter to ride them to places unknown while I clutch and shift the magic stick."

"You still ain't no good, cuz, a ride and a stick has always been what you been about," said Louise, and Skeeter replied, "Well, somebody got to give these girls something to smile about. Besides, all they got 'round here is church and shoutin'. And after the shoutin', a little love screaming in the backseat of my car calms 'em right on down and gets 'em ready for another week diggin' taters, croppin' 'bacca, and still be broke this time next week. So, cuz, every lady needs a 'Skeeter' like me," he said laughingly.

Louise turned the conversation into another more serious matter. She started to tell Skeeter that she had been thinking some matters of business that required her to have a partner that she could totally confide in, and it was most important that her name remains hidden from the public arena. She continued to unfold her business plan by stressing in the preface that her plan involved having a partner who not only could be trusted but also was cunning, smooth, and focused on reaching the desired results. Skeeter pressed Louise to get to the plan because he assured her that he could be trusted, and he was convinced nothing could further soil his reputation. "Cuz, if you need to explore the black market business, I am your man. You know, I have spent all of my adult life hustling. I know how to roll in street life. In fact, I'm not comfortable in anything else," said Skeeter.

"OK, cool," said Louise. "I'll just lay it out to you, cuz, and tell me what you think."

Skeeter said, "Cool." Louise started by telling Skeeter that she was the quiet mistress of Colonel Johnson and that she had been for nearly twenty years. "That's one of the reasons I was given the best shack on shack row." Skeeter said, "Cuz, I knew that already, so what's up now?"

Louise said, "That's just the beginning of it. I'm cool with it because the colonel has been very good to me and my kids. But sometimes, he has me to provide company with some of his business friends and keep them happy when they are visiting." So Skeeter said, "OK, cuz, you want me to kill him or what?"

"No," Louise said. "I found out that when I give company to his friends, he is the one who gets paid. I don't get a dime for it, and my actions are very important in the business transaction. So I started thinking maybe I could put together my own side of business providing company to some rich white men. I'm talking about just a few who think I'm pretty, and I can show them I'm safe, and their personal business with this black beauty is secure. Now that's just part of my idea. Next, and this is where you are very important, we can open a spot in the empty house down from where you live, and we can sell some hooch for those who can't get around much because they do not have cars. And we can sell it on credit, so at the end of the week, the drunks will owe most of their checks to us."

"Now, you'll need a big strong dude who can help keep the customers in line. Do you know anybody like that?" Skeeter said. "I have a partner I met in prison, and he's looking for something, and this certainly fits in his skill set. And he is cool. He goes by the name of DC."

"OK," said Louise. Louise continued to unfold her intricate business plan, which would provide logistics in implementing this enterprise. Her plan to make all this run smoothly hinged on her beauty and brains. She was very popular in the church and community with amazing influence because of her incredible singing voice. And it was important to her to keep that intact. Her children were very proud of her, and they were so happy to hear members of the church and community discussing the very special talent their mother, Louise, possessed.

Louise understood her mission very well. Her goals were to make more money, protect her children, protect her reputation, and make sure the powerful Colonel Johnson knew nothing about it. To pull all these off required organization and clarity of roles for all participants.

After sharing the mission with her cousin Skeeter, she became confident, and it prepared the way to implement her plan. She told Skeeter he needed to get started while she felt she was still marketable.

The next day, she went to work as usual but asked Mrs. Ellie if she could use the phone because she wanted to make a call to New York to check on her sick aunt. Mrs. Ellie was quite unsuspecting of Louise's real purpose to use the phone, which was to call Mr. Charles Burnhart, who was a city councilman and had experienced the pleasure of Louise's company arranged by Colonel Johnson some months earlier. She wanted to call him for several reasons. First, she remembered how fond of her he was and remembered him saying that anytime she wanted a better life, he would avail himself in helping her. Secondly, Councilman Burnhart was rich, proud, and underhanded, and he loved beating the system for profit. Thirdly, he believed in making lots of money by any means necessary. And lastly, Louise's company of pleasure was actually second to his desire to have her love. This understanding, she fancied, would serve as a foundation for her to implement her private business of pleasure and lascivious communion.

When Mr. Burnhart received the call from Louise, it was just as she suspected. He was immediately thrilled to hear her voice and quickly agreed to meet her the same evening to discuss these matters of great interest.

Skeeter's role at this point was to pick up Mr. Burnhart and take him to Louise. It would be late in the evening, and Dominique and her baby sister, Lorraine, would be fast asleep. The night finally arrived when Mr. Burnhart would meet Louise. When he entered Louise's house, she began stripping off her clothes right in front of him, and her stunning beauty consumed him, and the flame of sensual desire erupted in his veins until he could hardly contain himself. So struck was he at the thought of her being in his arms, nothing she asked would have been denied.

Louise's artful methods of pleasing men were all on full display, and Mr. Burnhart's world was turned upside down. His physical responses were reminiscent of someone having an epileptic seizure. His speech, seemingly incoherent, resembled the ecstatic fire that comes from an encounter with the Spirit where moans and groans are uttered in "cloven tongues"; and although still connected and cognizant of being limited by both space and time, there was a part of his psyche that thought perhaps heaven itself could not rival this moment of ecstasy.

After he collected himself back into sanity, he handed her $250 and his private phone number to his office while simultaneously pledging resources and support to her. Skeeter took him back to his office so he could get his car and go home. But just before departing, he told Skeeter to take care of Louise because she was very important to him. Skeeter agreed to do that and told Mr. Burnhart good night.

Skeeter returned from his trip to Mr. Burnhart's office to find Louise in seventh heaven. She told Skeeter the amount she was given, and they both celebrated because $250 a month in 1947 was good for an average black family. But for thirty to forty minutes of work, it was literally out of the question. This

AS NIGHT FALLS | 7

arrangement went on for about six months before Louise sensed she could take it to another level.

Most would have been quite satisfied with this extra $250 every week, but not Louise. She still wanted more. She thought she needed one more client like Mr. Burnhart. Then she could finance the hooch business she envisioned. But never would she share that with Mr. Burnhart because she knew his feelings for her ran deep. In fact, her name for him was "Lovestruck Burnie." Burnie's consistent giving to Louise was wonderful, she thought, but one more similar to him would be fantastic.

Although she was eager to put in place at least one more client to push her jewels, she was optimistically cautious to whom or when she would be able to implement her next gold mine. For now, she had decided in the short term to keep things as they were because "Lovestruck Burnie" was falling more deeply in love. So this arrangement remained for another six months. Each Tuesday night at 11:30 p.m., Skeeter would pick up client Burnhart and deliver him to his weekly sessions of unbridled pleasure.

Now a complete year had passed, and the comfort level for Louise had risen. She felt confident in pushing Burnie into giving her more assistance, so she planned well their next encounter. This time, for the first time, her session of pleasure rendering would include music from the radio, a scrumptious meal with candles, and Louise decked in heels and a seductive see-through gown in order to convince Burnie that it was not just business for her, but she too was falling in love with him. Burnie showed up and was overwhelmed with passion and desire for Louise, so much so that he told her his love was real and that this commitment was for life. He continued to tell her that although he was married with two kids, he could no longer see himself as living without her. Louise saw Burnie's sincerity and was extremely sure that she now had him where she wanted him. Louise kissed Burnie on his lips, which served as a prelude for what was about to happen. She took his hand and placed it on her hip and said, "All this is for you."

Burnie sighed and said, "What in the world have I done to deserve such a feminine delight?"

She then blindfolded him and led him into her bedroom and said, "Wait before you remove the blindfold. Just listen to the music as I read something for you, daddy. Now you know I'm a church girl, and I wanted someone special to express my feeling tonight." She started to read, "Set me as a seal upon thine heart, as a seal upon thine arm: for love is strong as death; jealousy is cruel as the grave; the coals thereof are coals of fire, which hath a mast vehement flame." (Song of Solomon 8:6).

Burnie was again immersed in a sea of her love. She asked him to get ready for her, so she took off his blindfold, and he beheld the rose petals on the floor and in the bedroom, and he was totally hypnotized by her seductive spell. When pleasurable exhaustion had consumed his body, and his pulsating veins and racing heart started to subside to normal rates, his mind and thirst for her love became fixated and insatiable. At this special moment, which was well orchestrated and calculated by Louise, she presented a program which would augment his giving to her. She mentioned that she was trying to attain a better life for herself, and the idea she wanted to pursue was black market alcohol, but she needed a vehicle to pick up and transport the hooch.

Burnie said, "That's no problem, sweetheart. All I want you to do is be careful and take care of my heart." She said, "Burnie, your wish is my command."

Burnie said, "Have Skeeter to meet with me tomorrow at City Auto Sales and I'll buy a truck, and he can bring it to you. Does that make you happy, darling?"

"Oh, Burnie, I love you," said Louise. Burnie began to cry with joy, so she hugged him and wept. After Burnie redressed, he summoned Skeeter to get ready to take him back, while Louise smiled with an expression of great appreciation, which actually served as veneer to the cold, callous heart and the special art of deception she cleverly possessed.

When Skeeter returned from taking Burnie back to his office, his cousin Louise told him to start cleaning up the old house because they'll have a truck soon to haul their hooch. But Skeeter said, "Cuz, where are we going to get the hooch from?" Louise assured him she had a plan for that, but it will require another midnight client, and she was on it at a distance for now but was setting up things every day, getting ready to make her move.

The next Sunday was particularly special at church. Louise performed two solos before an emotionally charged congregation, and seemingly, every eye in the place was moved by the Spirit. Her second song was "Precious Lord, Take My Hand," and as she sang, it was though her eyes were affixed in the presence of God. One after another fell under the power of the Spirit, and as they lay prostrate on the floor, Louise interjected a personal testimony of how the Lord had kept her through dangers seen and unseen. The song was extremely moving, but the insertion of her sermonic material into her musical presentation seemed to connect with everyone assembled in the place. What was unusual this day was even Skeeter was crying and rejoicing over the move of God. When church was over, Louise, Skeeter, and the kids went home for dinner. There was great silence on the ride home. The silence seemed to be very loud, rebuked of their private enterprise. When they arrived home and the kids went out to play, Skeeter asked Louise if she was OK, and she responded, "Yes, I'm just fine." He said that after the service today, he thought she was going to bail out on what they had started. She quickly retorted, "No, fool, church is one thing, and I love it. But business is business, cuz."

That Sunday was unusual indeed. The pastor stopped by to visit with Louise that afternoon to congratulate her on her incredible rendering of music at services earlier. He continued to point out to Louise that her special anointing would also serve as a glaring light that would cause her to stand out and make her more of a target for Satan to seek out, kill, and destroy.

"Amen!" said Louise. And she continued to share with the pastor how each day she wakes up, she prays with her children and anoints them to protect them from the evil that exists in the world.

"Praise the Lord, Sister Louise. We are so blessed to have you in our church," the pastor said.

"No," replied Louise, "I'm blessed to be a part of the church because life is tough for me and my children, and sometimes I wonder how I'm going to make it. But somehow, God makes a way for me, and sometimes it's through unusual events." The pastor replied, "Well, sister, God's ways are not our ways." And Louise said, "That's right, Pastor! And that means to me also that He brings some blessings that might be wrapped in strange paper."

"So true," said the pastor. The pastor then prepared to depart and ask if he could pray with her. She graciously agreed. When the pastor finally left, Skeeter entered the house and asked, "What's up, cuz? I stayed away because I saw the pastor's car here." She said, "He's such a fine man, and I enjoyed him coming but needed him to go because the colonel wanted me to stop by this afternoon. Mrs. Ellie is away with her sister in Philadelphia, so he wants some hot chocolate before he goes to sleep, and he seems to love the way I fix it (wink, wink)."

"How old is the colonel?" asked Skeeter.

"He's around seventy now," said Louise.

"Wow!" Skeeter responded. "He doesn't look it at all."

Louise said, "Trust me, ain't nothing old with his game. He can play as hard as any of them. Anyway, I got to go for a while. You take care of my girls for me and don't bring any of the easy women you deal with to my house. OK?"

"I got you, cuz," said Skeeter. When Louise got to the colonel's for what she thought was the usual purpose, it wasn't at all the case. He wanted Louise to meet Mary Mae Washington, who was also attractive and in her thirties. They met, and the three of them began to talk about many subjects. The colonel saw that it was getting late and asked Louise if she knew why she was called today. She said, "Not really." The colonel said, "Well, I have been hearing about how special you were in so many areas, so I thought I would have you and Mary Mae get familiar with each other in a biblical sense tonight while I give a play-by-play commentary for my good buddy William Robertson, whom we call Billy Bob. You girls might be able to figure out what to do and make it exciting and pleasurable. Louise looked at Mary Mae and said, "Are you OK with this?" Mary said, "Well, it's different for me, but I don't think it'll kill me." Louise whispered as the colonel left to get the phone to call Billy Bob so as not to miss a single section of the event. "Let's do what we got to do to get what we need. Besides, neither one of us could tell anything about the other. Furthermore, I got a plan. We'll pretend like we are really enjoying each other for a minute, then invite him to join us. We'll then blindfold him, and while you are working him, I can go in the closet where he stashes his dirty money, and I'll pick a hundred, and we can split it when it's over. Just trust me, I have been cleaning this house for twenty years, and I know where everything is. Besides, if both of us are serving him, and make sure he drinks, his mind will leave him and belong completely to us. We can do this, girl," said Louise. Mary said, "Come on, let's rock and rob, girl."

As the colonel consumed much alcohol, his behavior revealed that he was clearly out of touch with what was happening around him. He was not able to recognize who was who and was simply reaching for anyone who appeared before him. Louise felt that the time was right for her to make her move of thievery when there appeared to be a knock at the door. Unsure of what to do because no one was expected, nobody answered the knock, but the visitor continued to knock. Louise became irritated by the knock and told Mary Mae she would answer the door since she worked at the house and would try quickly to get rid of them. When she answered the door, it was Billy Bob who had waited to hear the threesome in action over the telephone, but the call was never made, so he thought something was wrong. Unbeknownst to Louise and Mary Mae, the colonel had counted his stash; and since he was going out of town early in the morning, Billy Bob was there to pick up the money to deposit it in the bank for the colonel, and any shortage would create great suspicion. That would have stripped them both of their favor with the colonel and certainly would have ended the dark business for Louise. Since now Louise was not able to complete her plan, she thought the next best thing was to show false affection for Billy Bob in an attempt to convince him that she really had secretive feelings for him. This pleased Billy Bob and was completely convinced when she flirtatiously blew him a kiss and placed her finger to her lips as a sign to him to "shush, it's between you and me." Billy Bob got her number and asked her to call him sometime. She said, "I will." Mary Mae then said to Louise, "I guess our moment is over now, but I did have fun with you anyway." Louise said, "It was OK, but nothing is good without getting some money from the deal. I am heading home now and will work on some ideas because you have to get money for this because the season is ripe!"

When Louise arrived home, she found the girls fast asleep and Skeeter lying on the couch, listening to Amos and Andy on the radio. Louise told Skeeter that he could go now because she was back and had some thinking to do. Skeeter was somewhat perplexed but left as Louise had instructed. Louise's thinking was centered on how she could get Billy Bob to play ball with her and be the other patron she needed that would give aid to building a greater financial base. Money was still needed to implement the second half of her business venture. And time was moving rapidly and she felt since more than a year had passed already, she thought she needed to make her move quickly but still very unsure how she would be able to pull it off. She knew that she had to overcome some obstacles to even introduce the idea of offering pleasure to Billy Bob and convince him to give her money in exchange for these moments of pleasure. Billy Bob, after all, was a deacon in the local church and a business partner of the colonel, was married with children and grandchildren, and was the host of a popular radio program in the Delta that discussed politics, religion, education, and what is called "appropriate social order of the day," which was very important during this Jim Crow Era of racial segregation. He also was a major voice in the Delta that vehemently spoke against sexual and social intermingling of different races. He believed both races would be destroyed if this practice was permitted by society. Week after week, his column appeared in the local newspaper where his venom was presented, and it infiltrated the psyche of the community.

With all these standing in Louise's way to convince him, her services were worth his altering his public persona and embracing the opportunity to feed and nurture his carnal appetites. After all, and above all, Louise believed in the weakness of men, and the power and hunger of the flesh craves to just feel good. This was her mind-set toward all men.

She also believed, given his public image, her approach to him would have to be shrewd and cunning. So after weeks of pondering her approach to lure Billy Bob into her fulfillment, she called him; and while he was cordial and courteous, she did get the impression that he was open to any intimate relationship with her. She was not very happy with the reception he had given, so she abruptly asked him if he found her attractive, and he quickly responded in the affirmative. What was then very confusing to her was why he was not pursuing her. After all, this was certainly what she was used to, and she thought he understood at least on some basic level what the call was about.

She continued to press him for more information as to why he seemed a little distant and unwelcoming to be sexually intimate with her. His seemingly new position was based on the fact that he had time to think and consider the whole matter and concluded it was not in the best interest to engage in this endeavor. He assured her that his decision was not based on any deficiency in her, but rather, he thought it was just best to abstain. Louise thought, *If this is the way you want it, that's the way it would be.* But she continued to tell him that she wanted to be close to him, and all she wanted from him was for him to help her financially as she sought a better life. Their cleverness would remain between the two of them.

He responded, "Oh, you want me to fund an enterprise of prostitution? Never!" Louise said, "That's not what I call it. I simply call it fun and finance." "Fun for you and finance for me. I have been in the church my whole life and have been happily married and upstanding as a Christian citizen for forty-one years, and I'll never participate in your evil. I never have, and I never will. And please know that no ignorant colored cleaning woman is going to take me into some low-down scheme and rob me of my money. You really must be crazy, girl," he said angrily. "OK, Mr. Whiteman," said Louise. "My problem with you white folk is we supposed to have nothing, and y'all supposed to have everything. Well, before you leave, I got one thing to tell you. I tried to have some leisure in a private business and personal affair, but you ain't got to do that at all. But please know the little Mr. Clean image you got with your church members and other white folk is going down the toilet." Billy Bob said, "What in God's name are you talking about?" Louise said, "Do you know Kathrine Washington?" Billy Bob was quiet and had a surprised look on his face. Then Louise said, "Don't get quiet or dumb now. Did you know Ms. Katherine Washington?" Billy Bob said, "Well, I'm not sure. It seems like the name does ring a bell." Louise said, "It should ring a bell because years ago, while you were singing in your church choir and having dinner with your wife and children, you managed to sneak out and ring Ms. Katherine's bell on the regular. She had a child that you fathered thirty-five years ago. Her name is Mary Mae Washington, and I know her well. Ms. Katherine told her that her father was dead, and she took the secret to her grave. The way I found out was in a Bible that was tucked away, buried under loads of boxes in a closet that she kept putting off, destroying the information, and she died before she ever did. Also, there are letters you wrote her, and you signed them 'Your eternal love in the shadows, Robby.' I can tell you more. Each birthday of Mary Mae's, you would wish her 'Happy Birthday' on your radio program and say this is from Katherine and Robby, and Katherine wrote it in her Bible every year for twenty-five years. So listen, mister, any way you want to do it, I can do it." Now Billy Bob started to tear up, and Louise said, "OK, you have two choices. We can lay and play, and you pay, or we can set up a 'you pay' system. You decide." Billy Bob suddenly had a change of mind and said, "I think the first way works better. Besides, entertainment is better than enlightenment in this instance." Louise said, "I agree." Now Billy Bob's attitude was extremely pleasant. He thought, *Well, Louise is an incredibly beautiful woman, and her company just might serve well*. Billy Bob said, "There's only one thing we need to discuss." Louise said, "What is that?" Billy Bob said, "On Tuesday nights, my wife and I have our weekly date, so that's not a good day." Louise said, "That's OK because I have choir rehearsal on Tuesdays. So I tell you, just in case your date night becomes an involved one, we can arrange Thursdays, and you would have a night of rest before our meeting." "That's just fine, Louise," said Billy Bob. "We'll speak again tomorrow." "OK, have a good one," said Louise. "I plan to, especially on Thursdays," Billy Bob said, smiling.

As night falls . . .

Louise was very pleased at the arrangement with these two men of the community. She glowed in the new enterprises that were running in full swing. Skeeter and his friend from prison were operating the hooch business, and every night, patrons from the Negro community flooded the house of drunken pleasure. And just as Louise had predicted, the men would come each night to wind down from their tedious and laborious task of manual work. The atmosphere was just perfect as they thought. They were drinking and smoking and many times would meet some of the young curious ladies who craved social entertainment.

The area was almost devoid of social establishments for Negros, so Louise's house of social outlet was an immediate success. Things couldn't be better for Louise. Her name was still kept from the ownership of this drinking joint, but she was truly taking full advantage of the profits.

Skeeter was very busy keeping things in place and making sure they ran smoothly. There he was running the hooch operation, and each Tuesday evening, he would meet "Lovestruck Burnie" and deliver him to Louise and stay close until approximately an hour later and take him back to his car. Then again every Thursday night about the same time, he would meet Billy and do the same. Louise was making an incredible amount of money from the two businesses, but as she made more money, there existed a problem in keeping it hidden and away from the eyes of the white community. She understood that she couldn't keep the money in a bank because there was no legitimate way to explain it, and that would not serve her interests well at all.

So she bought a safe and had a wall built to hide it in her closet. She trusted no one with the combination and immersed herself in the endeavor of storing more and more money into her secret bank. She managed to keep her lifestyle modest so as not to bring any unwanted attention to herself. She was rolling and rolling well.

After about two years of maintaining this system of operation, Louise had amassed nearly $100,000 in her private bank. Meanwhile, Billy's wife was starting to ask questions about his disappearances each Thursday night, but Billy seemed to manage the frequent inquisition of his wife rather easily, or so he thought. Within the next three months, Billy's maid was moved by her children up north because they felt their mother was getting too old for work and thought that after forty years, their mother needed to retire and take it easy. There left a vacancy in Billy's home and employment pool, and Louise thought it would be a great spot for herself because Billy was paying more than the colonel.

Also, when she discussed this possibility with the colonel, he gave his blessings because he told her Dominique was old enough to take care of the house for Mrs. Ellie, and it seems to be a fit for everybody. The next day, Louise went to Billy's house to meet his wife and family, and everybody seemed happy to have Louise as their new maid. Billy's wife, Margaret, was excited and impressed with the work of Louise, so much so that she invited Louise to travel with the family on weekend trips. Margaret would buy Louise new outfits and sometimes new dresses for Dominique and Lorraine. Again, Louise had struck gold. Everything was smoothly running just the way she wanted it, and she had finally felt nothing could stop her now.

At the same time, Dominique, though young, was enjoying her job at the colonel's home. She remembered her mother telling her years earlier to simply do whatever the colonel asked her, and it would be all right, and she would have good things in life. Well, it wasn't long before the colonel was ready to augment Dominique's duties to include providing him oral copulation behind the barn about once a week. Trying hard to be obedient and feeling she really had no other recourse, she would acquiesce to the colonel's desires. She was very loyal and discreet for about a year until she asked for more money but was told she couldn't get more money for the extra duties assigned.

The colonel said, "Dominique, you are a pretty colored girl, and you need to learn this now. You just supposed to do what white men tell you to do. That's what niggra girls are for. You were born to clean houses and be ready to pleasure white men when they take the notion." Dominique was furious and started thinking of some evil dark way to address the colonel's comments in unmistakable defiance. She felt demeaned and thought because she was a young black girl in the Deep South, no one of any real significance would even raise an eyebrow at the comments of the colonel. And at this very moment, Dominique believed his words represented the mind-set of the Deep South in general.

She felt powerless without any real weapon upon which she could rely but resisted becoming angry and responding out of misguided emotion. She thought it was better if she responded out of methodical thought. Dominique, though young, had mastered the idea of compartmentalization. She had come to understand it's not wise to bite the hand that feeds you even if you can't stand the hand. At present, she was not sure what she would do, but she had resigned herself to patience and believed that through it, she would find her answers. So for the time being, Dominique would continue, without contesting, to provide the colonel the fulfillment of his lewd and carnal desire, though unwelcomed and demeaning.

While young Dominique struggled trying to make it while enduring the pain of abuse from the colonel, things couldn't have been better for her mother. Louise was really enjoying the prosperity and control she had always envisioned. Her partners in crime were completely loyal to her. Her two private sponsors were extremely committed to her and her causes. Louise was not only gifted in singing, she had a most incredible way of persuading people to love her while protecting her from any negative reports. Not only was she protected by her inner circle, she was also envied by the other women in the community.

They never saw her publicly with a man, while every man around seemed to admire her enormous talent, God-given beauty, and style of elegance. Coupled with all that, Louise was not one who shared her personal life with those in the community; and while so many in the community were constantly struggling and complaining, Louise never did. The problem with all this was nobody around her could seem to figure out how she was doing all this. The jealousy made its way to the church and subsequently the choir. Now the joy on Sunday morning during worship became the rumor mill of presupposition with attached salacious lies about her as her critics and enemies continued to concoct fables that rarely resembled possibility, not to mention reality. The stories went from Louise and her pastor robbing houses together in neighboring towns, to her being the Black Ma Baker knocking over banks, who just hadn't been caught. And of course, when all else fails, it was common to go down the "Black Magic" road of putting roots on people to control their actions, leaving them impotent of employing their own mind in making decisions.

Louise continued to operate as if nothing was going on around her. She was only focused on making money. As long as the money flowed, all was well. Somewhere along the way in Louise's life, she became convinced that money could fix and solve everything. The only Bible verse that rose above all others was "a feast is made for laughter, and wine maketh merry, but money answereth all things" (Ecclesiastes 10:19). This was her true belief, especially the last part of the text. It was her succinct belief that money was truly the answer to all things. This was completely verified when one of the influential leaders of the church insisted on stirring in the rumors surrounding Louise. This particular gentleman was renting a small house from one of the affluent white men in the city and was chronically falling behind on his rent obligation. Louise found out that her fellow church member was building a coalition against her to have her removed from the choir, so she approached the owner of the property and offered him $7,000 for the small house, and the owner said absolutely yes. But the owner inquired, "What would become of the tenant?" Louise answered that she would look after the tenant because he was a member of her church.

This pleased the seller, and the deal was done. The following Sunday, Louise met with her adversarial member and told him she was his new landlord and presented him the legal papers as proof. She continued to advise him that he had a choice to make from the following: "If you continue to harass me, then (a) your rent will go up $60 for the next two months and $90 by the third month; (b) your rent would have to be paid in full by the second of every month, and no late payment would be accepted under any condition; or (c) your rent would not be increased on this property because I'll decide I no longer want to rent my property, and anything left in the property five days from that day would be burned with the house because I would decide I want my land clear and devoid of a dwelling. So you decide, sir, which one would you like?" He tearfully said, "Please, Ms. Louise, don't uproot my family. I have nowhere else to go. If you let me stay, I'll forget all of this stuff and would see to it that it never comes up again."

She said, "Fine," and hugged him with compassion and whispered softly in his ear, "Go and get yourself together for worship, and remember, don't mess with a nigga woman with an attitude because I could remove your marbles, and you'll be left with only a hood because you your man would be all gone. Are we clear, sir?" "Yes, ma'am," he replied. "Yes, ma'am."

As Louise prepared for worship, that Sunday proved to be a coming-out party for Dominique. The congregation was prepared to hear Louise perform, which was congregationally desired and expected. But this particular Sunday, it was Dominique who put her enormous singing talent on full display. Most knew she sang well, but it had been some time since she had performed soloistically. Since the time she was last heard singing on the church choir, she was a very young child. But she had matured vocally, and the special unique sound her mother possessed could not compare with the vocal sounds she could produce.

That Sunday, her rendition of "Blessed Quietness" was as moving as any musical presentation her mother had ever given. The response she received from the congregation convinced her that her time had come. Although she was quite comfortable living in the shadows of her very popular mother, she also was in touch with her own skill and understood if she were smart, she could move her life to a wonderfully economic place. But now she knew she had to deal with a life of challenges.

Meanwhile, Billy continued to follow Louise's instructions. Each Thursday night, without exception, he found himself in the car with Skeeter, and ultimately in the bedroom of Louise, and subsequently forking over the $250 of fees required by her. As she continued to raise more and more money, she became daring. She began insisting that Billy take care of other needs in her house in order that the money she made in her sex business would not need to be used. Billy initially was not happy with this added demand for money, but he felt the risk of not complying was not worth the possibilities of the damage that could result from not doing so.

And each week, Louise happily tucked away her profits from these lewd enterprises; and with great excitement each Sunday, she sang and praise God vociferously. Everybody who worshipped there seemed quite moved by her presence and gifts. Each following Monday for Louise was business as usual. Just as she wooed the church crowd each Sunday, she was just as effective in charming Margaret, her employer. After years of balancing a life of holiness and lewdness, the money flowed, and a sense of invincibility surfaced with each passing year. As Louise's comfort continued to rise, the plight and struggle also continued to rise with her daughter, Dominique. The struggle turned. After Louise felt the pain that existed in her daughter's life, she felt that her motherly instincts and love should come to the rescue of her aching daughter. So after hugging her daughter and telling her she loved her, Louise told Dominique to not worry about anything because she would take care of the colonel.

That very night, after "Lovestruck Burnie" left, Louise called Skeeter back to the house for what she called a business meeting. Skeeter agreed to the meeting but thought it was just another meeting similar to the other ones. But this time, Louise told Skeeter she wanted to have the colonel killed because of the way he was doing Dominique. Louise thought there was nothing wrong with the oral copulation Dominique was providing the colonel. Her issue was what it had always been—the money.

Skeeter said, "OK, cuz, what you want me to do?" Louise replied, "Get up with DC and you guys take him out. But before you do, I want us to rob him and give half to Dominique for her stress over this." Skeeter said, "Cool, me and my boy will handle things at your word." Louise said, "Cuz, what in the world would I do without you?" He said, "You know us, cuz, we got each other's back, always." Louise and Skeeter ended their private meeting, but the meeting was overheard by Dominique who was thought to be fast asleep but clearly was not.

The next night after overhearing her mother's private meeting with Skeeter, Dominique wanted to talk to her mother about what was about to go down. She told her mother that she did not want her, Skeeter, and DC to get into trouble because of her. She told her mother everything was OK, and she could deal with everything. Louise responded by saying, "Dominique, I gave birth to you, and no one is going to do you like that and live." She continued to reassure Dominique that this was a matter for adults, and she should just stay out of the way and do as she was told.

The lust for getting even with the colonel continued to fester in the heart of Louise, but her special gift of compartmentalizing again calmed her emotions, which would as usual provide her the mind to focus on the present moment of life. So she would go to work, perform her domestic duties artfully, and present herself as the docile and fastidious maid while nurturing the burning flame of violence and treachery because she wanted revenge.

As she worked, moving furniture to clean behind it, scrubbing floors until they seemed shining as new, washing clothes, hanging them to dry in the radiant sunshine, and preparing and serving meals, she would hear the ugly demeaning words describing the insolent niggers of the city. But she would manage to hum and quietly sing her way through the challenging days because deeply hidden behind the veneers of humility, there existed a cold, callous cunning mind with a plan to always get even and to ultimately destroy all enemies at the risk of her own demise. And at this point, one thing motivated her other than money and power, and that was stripping the colonel of wealth and health by any sneaky means necessary. But even as Billy and Margaret would sometimes speak despairingly remarks about her former employer, the colonel, Louise would most consistently respond, "The Lord made a great man when he made Colonel Johnson because the colonel took care of many colored folks, including me and my family." Neither her unspoken anger nor her unexpressed vile contempt was shared with an audience she did not totally control.

Her cordial and congenial manner of respect especially to her employer was always apparent, and this was one of her greatest attributes–to win over the support of associates that further fortified her popular character of purity. Her public image was impeccable and almost without flaws, while weekly, she raked in large amounts of money from the sex, liquor, and extortion business that she ran and controlled from the seat of evil, which seemed to glow brightest in the darkness of the night.

Dominique, who had by now quietly moved into the outer court of her mother's treachery and had gathered enough information to craft a credible and authentic narrative about her mother's affairs, was frightened by the intentions her mother had for the colonel. Although she was hurt and disappointed by the treatment of the colonel, her love for her mother was real. She clearly did not want her mother to be placed in the position of revenge because of her. Dominique began to plan of some way she could get revenge without involving anyone because although she was still a teenager, she had seen quite a lot and was very mature for her very young age. Besides, by now, Dominique knew her mother owned the after-hours liquor joint, and Skeeter was the front man. She also knew that Tuesday and Thursday night visits were made by two men whose voices from their sexual excitement, though tempered, would sometimes seep through the noninsulated walls that were erected throughout the poorly constructed house. Then there were the hands that would exchange money, which would sometimes take place at the front door as the men would leave each meeting, indeed with a good night kiss. All these had been viewed by Dominique, who was pretending to sleep, gazing through a thin crack that ran a few inches down the wall next to the knob. Dominique felt that her mother was in the dark shady business of prosperity plenty enough, and going deeper in would take her closer to her death.

Agonized over the possibility of Louise getting into deeper trouble, Dominique decided to take matters into her own hands and do what she believed adults should do, and that was to handle their own business.

After months of thinking, Dominique began to think more like her mother. She considered her mother the world's greatest thinker, especially when it comes to thinking dark thoughts and enjoying bright rewards. So Dominique began to believe that revenue should precede revenge, a model of thinking that reflected the mind of her mother, Louise, which now had become her modus operandi. Her plot started with locating the secret places the colonel hid some of his money. She started noticing his stash habits.

The money he made from his rental properties were always given in cash because he rented mainly to poor blacks and indigent whites, and neither had bank accounts. After he counted the money, he would simply put it in his safe. That was it. And as far as she could tell, there were no other safe guards in place. She carefully watched him, and when he had been drinking excessively, he would forget the combination, but he had it written on tape that was stuck on the safe's back. She waited till the first of next month when renters would pay their respective fees and thought this was a good time to implement her plan. It was his usual to desire Dominique's special sexual favors after he gathered the renters' fees for the month.

So Dominique waited and anticipated her services would be desired on this particular day. She carefully attended to Mrs. Ellie and made her comfortable on the couch because she wasn't feeling the best that day, but the good old colonel never felt better. There he stood in the tranquility of a peaceful day, a napping Mrs. Ellie, and all other servants gone for the day when he yelled, "Dominique, come on here, girl. Give me a shine," which was one of the code words for Dominique to perform orally on him. Dominique said, "OK, Colonel, sir, I'll be right there." So comfortable was the colonel in Dominique's responding as usual, he unzipped his pants and exposed himself.

As she entered the room, he saw her with a bottle of gin and said, "Put that gin down and get to work. I have everything nice and clean for you." She said, "That's nice, Colonel, but can't we just have a little to drink first? It will be more fun." The colonel said, "Well, OK, darling you are such as pretty darkie, and it looks like you have started to enjoy this stick." "I sure do," replied Dominique. As the colonel drank, Dominique, standing in front of him, began to fondle her genitalia and insisted that he continue to drink.

After the colonel was well saturated with the gin, Dominique seductively touched him all over his body, telling him how much power he had and that she was so happy to be his chocolate cake. The colonel, slowly melting into the wiles of this young beautiful queen of domesticity, began to look at the ceiling as if heaven were opened just for him. He leaned back, his eyes rolled back in his head, and he swallowed repeatedly as if he was consuming his favorite dessert. She lifted his exposed penis to her mouth and asked, "Colonel, is this what you want?"

He responded lustfully, saying, "Oh yeah, Dominique that's exactly what Big Colonel wants."

"OK, Big C, I hope you enjoy this as much as I do."

"Oh, baby," cried the colonel, "I will. I will."

"Close your eyes and Dominique will please you, Colonel."

"Go ahead, sweetheart," he said while closing his eyes.

As she lifted his excited genitalia with her hands, he started to groan with excitement and anticipated pleasure. Then she reached under the couch and picked up the hedge trimmers while moaning pretentiously, and she placed his testicles between the trimmers. He felt a cold piece of sharp steel, so he opened his eyes and saw his genitalia in the sheers and her other hand firmly gripping the handles. He yelled, "What are you doing, girl?" She replied, "Oh, Colonel, I'm just tired of acting like a nut!" Then she pulled together the sheers with all her might, and blood gushed from the colonel's groin as he yelled, screamed, and hollered. Unfortunately, the house was ten miles away from any other neighbor. As callously as her mother, she walked away from him, leaving him helpless and pained on the floor. She walked methodically to the safe, opened it, and took all the money that was in it. Mrs. Ellie, awakened by the wails of the colonel because of his bleeding genitalia, looked and saw the pool of blood surrounding the colonel as he lay barely moving because of blood loss. She was so traumatized she had a heart attack. She suffered with dementia, with no recollection of the event whatsoever. The colonel died from blood loss caused by the horrific act by Dominique, but the narrative crafted by the family was Mrs. Ellie, in a moment of unexplained rage, committed this terrible act, and the dementia she had was undisputable evidence that it was the only thing that could have explained this tragic event.

The bereaved family of the deceased colonel was stricken by grief. Instead of the usual three to four days of receiving family and friends to comfort them, it was extended to an incredible ten-day event. They gathered at the home of the colonel each evening, reliving the colonel's life and promoting the narrative that Mrs. Johnson was the culprit responsible for his death. Mrs. Johnson was confined to bed and shackled by a rope to ensure her safety. She mindlessly wandered all over the place while seeking answers to explain the massive turnout of people that congregated at the house each evening.

The day of the funeral was greeted by another incredible number of well-wishers and curiosity seekers, who gathered together at the local church. And during these eulogistic moments, Louise was asked to give remarks to seemingly illustrate the colonel's interests and attachments to the poor, oppressed, and black community. Louise, with her popular grace and charm, spoke glowingly about her former boss, calling him both a servant and a saint. She then tearfully shared special moments about special acts of benevolence the colonel performed for her family and suggested he was the vessel God used to rescue her family from many unbearable periods of great pain. The words she offered to many who assembled there for the services convinced all that they were sincere.

But what many did not know was that was the genius of Louise. She possessed great powers to persuade. Her greatest strength was to capture and lure the minds of the audience and direct them to embrace whatever she was offering. This day was simply another day, another opportunity for her to employ her gift and achieve her desired goals. Because she knew the colonel and his wife well, she thought this opportunity to give remarks would protect some of her private thoughts about the death. That's why she visited the home of the Johnsons every day during the period of grief and brought food with her. This was important so that she could influence the family to let her offer remarks about the colonel. By doing this, she fancied, she could guide or deflect any questions that would suggest any of possible scenarios that would explain what actually caused the colonel's death.

Louise in her heart of hearts felt like she knew what really happened to the colonel even though she had never been told. The look on Dominique's face was most revealing to Louise, and even when Dominique wanted to privately speak to her mother, Louise never accommodated it and would pacify her by saying, "It's all right, baby. I'll always protect you from anything or anybody. You are my flesh and blood." Somehow, these words, though repetitious and expected by Dominique, would comfort her and help carry her through that moment of insecurity.

After the funeral, Skeeter said to Louise, "Cuz, how did you get up there and call the colonel a saint when I know you hated the cracker?" Louise said, "I couldn't stand the sucker, but that was my business, not other people there. Cuz, you need to understand the issues about the colonel died with him. Now, we have to live among these white people, and I don't need any mess with them. Let your anger die with your enemy." Skeeter thought that was a heavy statement. It was at this moment that Louise knew, at least to some extent, her life would change. But more importantly, she became more conscious of her need to maintain her veneer that covered her selfish character. It was this exchange with Skeeter that convinced her to keep a grip on herself because the eyes of others were probing into their lives. But in Louise's mind, you do whatever was necessary to get you through the moment especially when your goals are clear, concise, and very self-serving.

The death, burial, and the dementia of the Johnsons were tragic indeed, but for Louise and Dominique, it was a crisis that cemented emotional bonds. Dominique was in need of direction as to what to do with the $15,000 stolen from the colonel's safe. Also, she was now an unemployed domestic worker with no apparent ideas of her next move. Each morning as Louise would go to work, there in her room would Dominique sit staring out into the seemingly miles of fields yielding various crops that were dotted with many black sharecroppers working the land all day long in vain less efforts to amass dollars, but most often, they were only successful in gathering dimes. The backbreaking task of fieldwork did not in any way appeal to Dominique, but she understood very well that employment and purpose were the tools to fix a broken life, even if they were only available on the wrong side of the law. Dominique had learned the art of pleasuring men during her stint as housekeeper for the colonel. She thought it was time to have a business meeting with her mother. When Louise sat with Dominique, something very interesting emerged from their meeting. Dominique wanted her mother to know that she had figured out what was happening on Tuesdays and Thursdays late in the night with "Lovestruck Burnie" and Billy Bob. Also, Dominque told her mother that since she was not working, she could also be used in the late-night pleasure business. Dominique thought she was ready and mature enough to handle the duties assigned in the effort largely because of her service to the late colonel Johnson. Also, Dominique had become concerned about her mother's long days of engagement trying to work and oversee the pleasure business and the after-hour liquor house with Skeeter. Furthermore, she surmised her youthful beauty and sensuality would be even more alluring to older gentlemen, which might aid her pilfering more money for rendered services. Louise initially was not pleased with the idea, but upon more careful reflection, she conceded that perhaps it would be a good idea because in her mind, more money meant more leverage and power. But what brought Louise to this conclusion was really something that Dominique reminded her in their conversation, which was, "Since you going to give it to somebody, you may as well give it to somebody who can do something for you." But the question now is how would her insertion be worked out with the established clientele, Dominique wondered. But as usual, Louise's quick analytical mind came fluidly to the rescue. She thought she would began with one of the gentlemen, and since it would be in the pitch blackness of the night, she would excuse herself to visit the bathroom, and then young Dominique would enter the room to take over the task of pleasure rending. Louise's scheme to enlist Dominique in this lewd activity was not what it appeared to be. What Louise did not share with Dominique was her diabolical plan to gather more negative propaganda about her distinguished clientele engaging in lewd acts with a very young black girl. She had not planned to use it, but she thought it might be helpful to have it.

As night falls . . .

On the following Tuesday night, Burnie arrived at Louise's house as usual. Louise was eager to try her new scheme of using her daughter, Dominique, to sexually tag team Burnie. If for some reason the scheme failed, Louise was prepared to submit the reason of prodigious love for her actions. She was ready to admit to Burnie that her love for him was so big that she would even permit her daughter to share the bed with him. She thought he would be so thrilled by the gesture that his already-generous giving would easily give impetus to an increase upon her request. All these ideas were preconceived and ready for implementation should the need arise. By now, Burnie had made his way into the dimly lit room of Louise. The candlelights were slowly flickering, and the music from the radio contributed to a wonderful atmosphere of romance. So Louise, employing her usual grace, style, and charm, slowly undid Burnie's tie, unbuttoned his shirt, relieved him of his shoes, and helped him out of his pants. She kissed him and caressed his body all over. She relaxed him until she felt he was under her spell. Then there was a great pause. Burnie, so consumed by her, was burning and yearning for more of Louise's smooth flesh pressing against his when she suggested that she extinguish the candles and remove the rest of her clothes because she told him, "Tonight, Big Burnie, we won't need candles because all the heat you'll need will come from the fire of my canal." "Oh my," said Burnie. "And if heaven is any better than this, only God should probably live there." As she put out all the candles, the room was totally black. No one could see their hand or any other part of their body. She told him to just lay and relax for a moment and listen to the music as she stepped to the door to make sure it was locked. As she left, her voice still being heard was an indication that she was only a few feet away, and then her voice was hushed, and the smooth young skin of Dominique was felt by the eager client. He was so into it that it did not seem to matter who it was. Dominique kissed his neck, caressed his groin, and performed oral copulation on him slowly and deliberately, employing the skills she learned from her oral service days with the colonel. Burnie could hardly contain himself. He moaned and groaned wildly, suggesting to her to please don't stop. Burnie repeatedly said, "I can't take much more. I'm about to bust," but Dominique continued the process, causing him to groan as she provided this special pleasure to him. By now, Burnie was about to climax without intercourse because of the stimulation and sensation Dominique was providing. He warned Dominique he was nearing climax, but young Dominique, unfazed by his warnings, continued her activity. Within seconds, Burnie reached ejaculation while wails of pleasure rang throughout the house. Burnie was so embarrassed that he started apologizing for his continual outbursts and told her, "You had never been like this before, and it was so wonderful I just couldn't help myself." Without uttering a word, Dominique left the bed at the bewilderment of Burnie. Only seconds later, Louise returned and asked, "Did you really like that, Burnie?" "Oh, honey, you are simply a goddess in bed." "That's what I want to be for you always," said Louise. Burnie, so captured by his new experience, paid $400 this time instead of the usual $250, much to the delight of Louise. When Burnie left, he kissed Louise and told her he loved her, and he felt he had been given a new lease on life.

Louise was thrilled at the outcome of her scheme and immediately asked Dominique what in the world did she do to Burnie. Dominique said, "Oh, Ma, you know the answer to that," as she smiled. Louise said, "I thought I knew, but obviously, I don't because he paid more tonight than ever. You young girls must have found a new trick that the older ones like me need to know about." Dominique said, "Ma, it's like this: When you find something that really turns him out, don't stop it. Be open to everything, and in the end, you'll get everything. I make sure that no man can find another me, and no woman can ever replace me." Louise was really impressed with Dominique's outlook on things and told her that she would do very well in this business. She wanted to know more about how she took care of Burnie. Dominique told her mother that her generation does not have any hang-ups and prides themselves on fulfilling the needs of their partner. Louise responded excitedly and felt that the two of them had formed a great partnership which would financially reward them for a very long time.

Aside from involvement in this secretive enterprise, Dominique, like her mother, was an extremely gifted singer, particularly of gospel music. And Sunday was an important worship day. It was Easter, and as expected, the church was packed with congregants. Both Louise and Dominique were featured soloists for the occasion. The church marveled at the melodious rendering of each of them. It was so beautifully presented that no one dared put one over the other. It simply was a magical moment, and all were moved by the ministering of their splendid music. Perhaps what stuck out more about Dominique was that she would ultimately become a minister of the gospel in the ecclesiastical sense. She seemed very insightful about the plight of poor people and was able to publicly connect with them. Dominique enjoyed the remarks and went home in deep thought about what this could possibly mean. She consulted her mother about what she felt was happening within her concerning the remarks the congregants made and what she felt was taking place in her when she would sing and minister to the people. Her mother calmly tried to assure her that it was simply the explosion of passion for singing and feeding off the energy of the people. She wanted her to know it had been happening to her for years, but she had been able to separate feeling from finance. The wise thing for anybody to do was to attend church but amass the cash at every possible moment. Although Louise had been singing for years, pouring out her energy before the community, and seeing many shout, praise, and fall out while she was singing, in the end, it had come to financial naught. She wanted her daughter to understand a black girl singing in the poor south would probably live and die having not moved up in life one iota. Her position was that no one should live like that, and the last thing she wanted was her daughter to suffer the pain of the typical black life generally associated with the Deep South ideology. But at the same time, the call to Louise's conscience, which usually received no answer; however, the probable ounce of wholesome motherly direction she possessed did at least manifest itself and came forth to embrace her daughter's fondness of church activity, if only for a brief moment.

In the meantime, Dominique embraced the church and its basic causes. She became so church conscious that she started to believe the Lord was calling her into the ministry, specifically in a pastoral role. But her involvement in this nefarious activity did not create any measurable conflict within her. She was very comfortable amalgamating the sacred with the secular.

As night falls . . .

While she is proceeding in taking the next steps to her ultimate calling, which was ministry, the rumors of violence began circulating around the club Dominique and Louise silently owned. Skeeter's girlfriend, whom he thought he could trust, implicitly had another dude on the side, and she constantly gave him many favors at the club including free alcohol and anything else that he chose. If he wanted to keep company with one of the young ladies in the back, he too would never be charged for the services. He and Millie kept their relationship private for fear of Skeeter's quick tempered wrath. Word got to Skeeter that she was giving away free liquor to this gentleman all night, and the gentleman was never charged whatsoever. She lied and said that he pays for everything he drinks. That provoked an argument between Skeeter and Millie. Millie, in her anger, spoke in embarrassing terms about Skeeter's very small genitalia.

"I was only one who would even consider a follow-up visit because you could never satisfy any woman. Maybe your mess quit working because of all that liquor you have put into you, but even that does not explain why all the rest of you grew except that pitiful manhood, so yes, I had to find a man I could feel instead of just using my imagination with you." The ego assault made on Skeeter was heightening his anger. While Millie continued insulting Skeeter, the laughter on the part of the patrons was proving to be very uncomfortable for Skeeter. And to add further insult to an already-injured ego, Millie's boyfriend grabbed his crotch and said to Skeeter, "It's cool little, brother. I'll let you borrow mine sometime!" The crowd erupted in great laughter. That single act seemed to take the matter to another level of disgust for Skeeter. While the crouch-grabbing boyfriend of Millie was in a laughing stupor, Skeeter reached inside his jacket and pulled out his .22-caliber pistol and began shooting the dude. He shot until there were no more bullets in the chamber. As the shooting started, the patrons, like a stampede of cattle, rushed to exit the building seemingly all at the same time. The screams, the trampling over any who fell in the way, seemed to be the primary interest of all who headed outside where they believed safety resided. Skeeter just shot as long as he could, and when the bullets ran out, he simply reloaded as quickly as a gun slinger from the old Western days of Jesse James. Millie's boyfriend lay on the floor screaming because of pain and reached out to anyone that would help, while Millie was trapped behind the bar where there existed no door that led to the outside. With a reloaded pistol, Skeeter began to shoot Millie. He kept squeezing the trigger, unloading six rounds at her, but she continued to walk through the front door. By this time, the patrons had left the building, but many congregated outside to see how this terrible scene would end.

As some ran to Millie, believing she would die any moment now, more bullets rang out, two more hitting her just before she collapsed to the ground. It was without a doubt who the shooter was because many saw Skeeter pull the trigger and shoot Millie in the back as he stood in an obvious rage and he lowered his weapon.

As night falls . . .

Skeeter, who had run the secretive and lucrative operations for Louise for years, had become the talk of the town. In the middle of the night, Skeeter, having just returned to some semblance of sanity, visited the home of Louise to inform her what had happened because he knew that news would find its way to her ears sooner rather than later. Stunned and mortified was Louise at this disappointing news. She cried and was visibly angry at the juvenile behavior of Skeeter. Louise could not believe Skeeter would go that far in his anger toward Millie or really anyone else. To Louise, Skeeter was a con artist, not a killer. She thought his lust for multiple women was so high that no one woman could move him emotionally, but obviously, Millie did. Louise, still upset over the event, wanted to know why he had to shoot so many rounds at these people. Skeeter told Louise two things guided his thinking. Skeeter said, "I shot that dude six times, and I shot Millie eight times because I meant to kill them. But I shot Millie more times than the dude because the tramp wouldn't fall. And when I shoot you, I mean for you to fall." But the drinking and gambling hot spot was on the verge of not being as lucrative anymore because this act of violence would uncover the scabs of a morally infected community and the residue it left behind.

Louise found herself in a place of great discomfort. The town continued to talk about it, and the local newspaper continued to investigate the story because historically, the town, though in the Deep South, was rather quiet; and while there was a racial divide, there were very little racial riots or fights. There just seemed to be an unwritten code of conduct between the races that existed without pronounced violence. But the nature of this event created a buzz, and more information was needed by the general public, and there was the issue of law. Louise wanted none of this because she felt if the powers get involved, that would turn the customers away. She clearly knew that her customer base wanted no dealing with downtown. Louise, though unhappy, knew she had to take care of the problem in some effective way. But her options were not very good, irrespective of which direction she would choose.

The first thought that presented itself to Louise as a starting point was to get her children out of town to protect them from the potential ugliness that would surround the investigation of the shooting at the club. Her younger daughter, Lorraine, who was a lover of knowledge, had graduated from high school at the top of her class and had been offered a scholarship to a northeastern university. Louise insisted that she leave now instead of waiting for the fall semester to begin. Louise thought she could stay with a cousin in Philadelphia for a couple of months. When mentioning this as a possibility of leaving to Dominique, the answer was a firm "no" because she wanted to be with her mother during this whole investigative process. Louise was greatly moved by the gesture of her daughter and was appreciative to her for that touching act. Although in her heart, she still preferred her to leave town.

But now the problem was front and center on her mind, and she knew that in order to maintain her image, she needed a plan. As she pondered, she recalled something an elderly man told her; and that was to win favor of the white community, you first need to obtain the favor of another white person. The light bulb came on. She thought, since she had two of the most influential and affluent men in town as midnight clients, she would persuade them to speak on behalf of Skeeter since he had been their pickup driver for years to their place of pleasure. So the very next night, she met Burnie. She appealed to his love for her to enlist his support and get the whole matter squashed. And by the time their evening together had ended, Burnie was down with the whole idea. Two days later, she met Billy Bob. Although Billy was not as in love as Burnie, his lust for her sexually had risen to such a height that he would have done virtually anything to keep her happy. So Billy was on board with using his influence with the district attorney in not pursuing any charges either. After presenting her idea to her clients and both lined up in support of Louise's plan, she felt much better now because she firmly believed what these two men said in that town was law and gospel.

While Louise thought things couldn't get any better given these circumstances, another windfall of luck bounced her way. After using both her charm and her body to persuade the two most powerful men in town to assist her with her plan to have the potential charges against Skeeter squashed, miraculously, both Millie and her boyfriend lived and wanted to press no charges against Skeeter. So Louise suggested to her sexual confederates that she understood the district attorney would continue to investigate the shooting, but she was sure no witness would come forward, and that should lead him to the idea that although something happened at the club, he'll probably not be able to prove his case. Both Burnie and Billy agreed and assured Louise it would be handled that way. Besides, blacks could not vote, and it was a black-on-black crime. Also, blacks had to pay poll taxes and pass reading tests. And very few could do either. Besides, only 3 percent of blacks were even registered to vote in the South anyway.

"Let's just leave this one alone," said Burnie to the district attorney. They strongly felt that since there appeared to be nothing to gain by pursuing charges against Skeeter, why waste the taxpayers' money on it. The district attorney's office closed the case without bringing any charges to Skeeter.

It was now time for Louise to regroup and for Skeeter to calm down his erratic temper and make the club a desirable place for the customers to return. It has been said the public has very short memory. And this was surely the case with this club. Within months, more staff was hired, including greater security. Drinking limits were imposed; however, any patron could still get wasted long before the drinking limit would have been reached. No arguing would be tolerated, and the bartenders worked in tandem instead of alone. The community was quieting down, and the good times at the club had made a full recovery. Skeeter became more active in church and started offering more help to people in the community. And happy days were here again!

Louise returned to work to resume her life and personal activities at Billy and Margaret's home. Her joy seemed to return, and her humming and singing as she worked had never sounded better. Getting back in the flow of her normal routine was quite satisfying, and worrying about her daughter, the club, Skeeter, and her special clients had completely subsided. She joked and laughed with visitors and guests each day. Her work ethic was again at its highest. She became much more meticulous in even the small tasks, and this was particularly pleasing to Margaret. Because she was so much more impressive, Margaret had decided to give Louise a raise, citing the fact that she surely deserved to be rewarded because of her careful attention to detail. Louise had become more and more comfortable with her job and began to think about having a long future with Billy and Margaret. The relationship between Louise and Margaret flourished with Louise's return to work. She always cared for Louise, but now she was truly connected to her and considered her to be a significant part of the family.

Within weeks, Louise and Margaret began to ride together downtown to shop, have lunch, and just hang out together. Sometimes, Margaret would insist that Dominique come along too because she had become fond of Dominique as well. Margaret would often tell Louise that given Dominique's talent and beauty, she should be exposing her to more refined activities. Louise was very grateful to Margaret for her care and interest in Dominique and suggested to Margaret that the next time she would be performing, she would love for her to come. Margaret was grateful and promised she would attend.

Amid this flowing love and new bonds of friendship between Margaret and Louise, Billy Bob was continuing his Thursday night visits to Louise's place and was enjoying himself more and more. His enjoyment was transforming itself into relaxed comfort. Virtually every day, as Louise would come to work, Billy would find a way to interact with Louise. It started with a quick kiss here and there, to a sexual remark, to a feel on her breasts. As the comfort levels continued to rise, Billy became more embolden in his aggression. Louise warned Billy to wait until they were alone at their usual Thursday night session, but the sense of control or arrogance grew more intensely in him. So he would look to ensure Margaret was not able to see either him or Louise, and he would insist on more passionately expressed moments with Louise on the back porch, behind the shed in the back, or sometimes in the kitchen while Margaret was taking a nap or otherwise engaged. This worked for months for Billy and Louise when an unexpected event caused things to turn in a whole new direction.

Billy's unchecked comfort created a great cause of concern when Margaret, relaxing on the sofa and listening to the radio, called Billy, whom she thought was in his study doing some paperwork, but he did not answer. Margaret just wanted him to rush to the radio and hear an advertisement about a new product she desired but couldn't remember the name. When she looked in the study and found he was not there, she casually walked toward the kitchen. She looked in and was shocked beyond belief. Billy was kissing Louise passionately. His hands were all over Louise's body. Louise was whispering, "Billy, we better stop before Ms. Margaret catches us." Billy responded laughingly, "Old girl is probably asleep now. You know by now she ain't much good when her gut is full." But it was hardly amusing to Margaret. She was extremely angry. Her first thought was to go in there, bust them, and with all the anger she could muster, fight and strike them both until she could strike no more. But immediately after her thoughts of violence, she gathered herself and thought that now was not the time. One very great consideration was if she left Billy, what would become of her life? After all, she was in the Deep South, and she had no visible means to maintain her lifestyle. And in the south during this era, many powerful men had private affairs with black women. It could be construed as just part of the social landscape. Although she was methodical, she was still mad. She felt like she had to do something but thought she would say nothing and gather more information to determine to what depth this had gone. Billy was unaware of Margaret's discovery, so he went about his business as usual. The following Thursday night, Billy took his bath which was his routine around seven o'clock that evening and announced to Margaret that this night would be another long business meeting with some church officials, and later, they would probably stop by one of the brothers' home for a friendly game of rummy. Margaret simply nodded her head, and he kissed her on the cheek and left. Margaret waited until she was sure he was out of sight and called her friend Florence Perkins from the missionary guild. She spoke with Florence about allowing her to use her car for a moment because she had a personal errand she needed to run. Florence allowed her to use her car but sensed anxiety in Margaret and inquired if everything was all right. Margaret quickly responded, "It's just fine, Florence, and I'll get you your car back to you tonight."

Florence said, "That's fine, Margaret."

When Margaret got the car, she really was unsure where to go and find Billy. So she went to the church and to some of his friends' homes, but Billy was not there. She rode around the town but could not find Billy anywhere. She was really confused now. All the diners in town either had closed or were about to close, and this became more confusing to Margaret. So she just drove on the outskirts of town to a diner to get a cup of coffee before heading back home with no apparent answers to her perplexing questions. As she got closer to the diner, she saw Billy's car. She decided to wait to see what would happen. After about an hour and a half, she saw Billy coming out of the diner and getting into a car with a black man. More perplexed than ever, she wanted to find out where Billy was going. She rode at a great distance behind the car and followed the car back into town. The car traveled across the railroad tracks that served as a divider between the black and white neighborhoods. At last, the car stopped at a shotgun house apparently owned by a black resident, and Billy emerged from the car while the black man remained in the car. As Billy approached the door of the house, Louise, dressed in a housecoat and high-heeled shoes, came out on the dimly lit porch. She hugged him as they entered the house, and she saw Billy's hand grip on Louise's behind, and within seconds, all the lights were turned off. Margaret observed the shocking scene for a moment and drove away consumed with anger, pain, and frustration.

Later that night when Billy returned home, Margaret asked him, "How was the meeting?"

Billy responded, "Never better, honey. I think our progress as a unit is really taking off."

Margaret answered, "I believe that it is because you really seem committed to this project, whatever it is."

"I am, darling." He went to kiss her cheek, but Margaret was slower in responding, but it was unnoticed by Billy. He said, "Good night, dear," and she just turned over to pretend she was going to sleep. But sleep hardly made its way to Margaret that night. She just lay there in the bed staring in the thick blanket of darkness, trying to manage her anger until she made her next move. All night, she waited on the dawn of the day so she could start addressing Billy's troublesome activities but knew she needed to do it carefully so as not to reveal what she had clearly discovered.

The next day, Margaret still found herself in anger because of the deceit she felt toward Burnie and the vile she felt toward Louise. She was so hypnotized by her rage that reason and logic were completely robbed of their presence. Death for Louise was the only conclusion Margaret could draw from the pain of deception she attributed to Louise. The only semblance of reason that appeared in Margaret's mind was to murder Louise without the bloody gruesome methods that initially saturated her psyche of her decadent destruction. So Margaret became determined to satisfy her lust for Louise's blood in a cold and callous way, employing deceit, deception, and detached betrayal. Besides, in Margaret's mind, "what goes around comes around." And spiritually speaking, that passage in the Pauline epistles of the Holy Bible seemed to fare well in this situation, which was, "God is not mocked; Whatsoever a man soweth, the same shall he also reapeth."

Two weeks passed, and the rage of Margaret's anger was still being fueled by the notion of getting even with Louise. The following day, Billy was preparing to go on a business trip, and he was getting things in order for his departure, and this included some personal contact with the authentic love of his life, Louise. Inasmuch as this was not the usual time for him and Louise to copulate at her house, he thought he could just have a quick moment with his private paramour out in the barn among the nonverbal observance of the livestock. When he whispered his intentions to Louise, she as usual availed herself to accommodate Billy's desires. Unbeknownst to Billy, his wife of several decades watched him like a mother hen watching her baby chicks. Each move Billy made, irrespective of how methodical or cunning, Margaret, with the slyness of a fox, watched, probably seeking additional fuel to assist her emotionally to execute her diabolical and dastardly act of cold-blooded murder. After the instructions were clear to Louise exactly what Billy wanted her to do, she eased out of the house on a rather-cavalier walk across the well-manicured lawn that carpeted the breathtaking landscape. She arrived at the barn and hid herself between bales of hay that were set aside for the nourishment of the herbivorous livestock. She removed her blouse, stripped off all other bodily clothing, and quietly moaned, anticipating the arrival of Billy as the unintelligible sounds from the cow's presence served as sounds of melody that created an atmosphere and ambiance for human copulation which always pleasured Billy.

As Billy made his way closer to the barn, he could hear the groans of Louise summoning him to come and mate with his mistress. Gone was Billy's youth, so running to her was not an option, but the excitement of sexual intercourse with Louise put an acceleration motion in the movement of his feet. Because Billy knew if he could make it to the place where lay his love, his vim, vigor, and vitality would truly be restored. He entered the barn, and immediately, with the exuberance of a young child unwrapping presents on Christmas Day, Louise began to relieve Billy of his clothes. She took him, kissed him, caressed him, fondled him, and positioned herself for him to engage in acts that had escaped Billy decades ago. He was seduced and beguiled, and every part of Billy's aging anatomy was kissed, licked, and taken in Louise's oral cavity like a newborn takes to a pacifier. Billy, so spellbound by the sexual gifts from Louise, uttered in the throes of sexual ecstasy, "I must be in heaven 'cause nothing on earth compares to this."

Margaret looked quietly at her husband wrapped up in Louise's world of newfound pleasure. The range of her emotions went from envy to disrespect. So scorned was she, the fury of hell could not compete with her thirst for retribution. Amid her hysteria, she was able to collect herself long enough to keep deeply buried her thoughts to destroy the woman she felt had alienated the affections her husband of many years had expressed to her.

As she moved farther away from the lustful, adventurous, and even theatrical scene, she began to speak aloud, "I have to kill her. I have to kill her." With each step, her voice was raised to higher decibels. "I must kill her!" And to provide herself greater comfort for the thought of murder, she began to say, "It's God's will for me to remove this menace to decency and this whore sent from hell to pollute the purity of God's superior race, the white people."

The next day, Billy loaded his car and headed out of town to his business meeting. The weather was sunny and balmy. It was St. Patrick's Day, and there was great enthusiasm in the city as the townsfolk was awaiting the festive celebration to begin. Although most employees gave their employees the day off, Margaret insisted that Louise report to work as usual but assured her the workday would be short and the workload light. Margaret expressed interest in wanting to have a brief celebration of St. Patrick's Day with Louise since Billy was out of town. Louise, the usually obedient employee, agreed to Margret's request but was not at all thrilled at the idea. She thought although it was not her desire, she could tolerate being with Margaret for a few moments to celebrate the occasion.

When Louise arrived at her place of employment, Margaret was already up and dressed. She was unusually happy and most hospitable to Louise. She instructed Louise to just relax, and she would not have to wash clothes or do any housework today. "Today," Margaret said, "would be a day of leisure and celebration." Louise, a little baffled by Margaret's behavior, did not question too much because she was thrilled at the idea of relaxing and still getting paid a day's wages. So Margaret gave Louise a drink of very expensive wine served in the formal glasses usually reserved for her white guests. Louise lost herself in the notion of experiencing a "white" moment. For the first time in her life, she felt, if only for a second, like she was socially equal to an affluent white woman. Never did she ponder the preposterous idea that she would be sipping wine from a long-stemmed wineglass. The wine to which she was accustomed was gulped from a glass jar with no label and with a twisted top which was very similar to a mason jar routinely used to preserve pears and jellies. But now with her pinky finger extended as she sipped from the glass, a feeling of social significance flooded her very being. One glass after another, she sipped quite comfortably with the idea that perhaps she had found a new friend in Margaret. Suddenly, Louise began to feel light-headed and dizzy. She tried to stand up but was unable to balance herself. Her stomach started to feel queasy, and nausea accompanied her already-fainting body. She tried to speak but couldn't seem to pronounce the words. The room was spinning, and her vocal chords were constricting, leaving her gasping for air. Her heart beat more and more rapidly as she continued to lose control of her muscles. She started to vomit and urinate as her bowels moved without command of them. Her body jerked in every direction as she faintly heard the laughter of Margaret. It appeared like she was having an epileptic seizure with yelling and screaming, but Margaret stood taunting her, saying, "I hope you die. Go ahead, you nigger whore, die. You need to die and all the rest of your kind. You have been drinking arsenic the last thirty minutes. What took you so long to start dying?" Margaret stood over the jerking body of Louise and said, "Before you die, I got to pee, and in your face I am going to pee. So die! This is the last drink you will ever have, so enjoy your death, tramp!" Without saying a word, Margaret sat down and had a glass of lemonade before she called EMS.

She was dead by the time they arrived, and they saw Margaret crying and displaying great grief. She continued to say loudly how she loved Louise and could not bear her death. She was so convincing. The EMS personnel tried to calm her and found some tranquilizers to help her rest. She, in her hysteria, repeatedly asked how she died. The EMS personnel responded, "Who knows. These people live very irresponsible lives, ain't no telling. But I'm sure it'll be considered 'natural causes.'" Margaret, fighting back tears, said, "I tried to do my part to make life better for all people, but I went out of my way for this one." Having said that, she was assisted to her bedroom where she retired for the evening.

After the funeral of her mother, Dominique's singing went to new levels. Each Sunday, the members of her church gathered to listen to the melodious sounds that came from the vocal chords of Dominique. As she sang, the inspiration of her words touched the hearts of those assembled. In fact, the morning message given by the pastor continued to fade into obscurity because of the anticipated and expected singing of Dominique. There seemed to be a definite turnaround in her spirit. Even as she walked the streets of the city, people would recognize her and interact with her as if she were a celebrity.

She seemed quite humbled by the kindness shown to her almost on a daily basis. But the most interesting part of her singing performances was her unique improvisation at interludes where she would insert the powerful and pervasive "preaching praise components" in her presentations. The congregation was more moved by her singing uniqueness than they were by the pastor's preaching of the word. This was not an occasional occurrence; it was a part of every song she performed. As time progressed, the preaching portions of her singing started to be longer than her singing of the songs. Her moving tones were backed by the choir and musicians in the traditional black church's interpretation of the Spirit of God taking over and consuming the presenter. It is during these times the congregants believed the preacher/singing was under the spell of the Divine. While under this spell, it was believed the preacher/singer would be able to receive great revelation from God and would therefore be able to address human issues and concerns that were of great value to the congregation. She would stir her words into melodies that moved the listener who had been religiously shaped by the tradition that accompanied blacks from tribal Africa to the foreign lands of America. Each word sang or preached, the musicians and choir would add similar tones immediately to ensure unity of thought and spiritual confirmation. Dominique led the congregation in this as the members would be taken to the lofty plateaus of the Divine Presence. None seemed better at this. Dominique was so talented and so endowed with stunning beauty the community considered her the queen crooner. Her popularity attracted men who desired her and women who simply wanted to be her. She quickly became the object of desire, jealousy, and envy depending on one's perspective.

While enjoying the popularity, she still felt grief from the death of her mother, the closing of the club, and the unawareness of Skeeter, her mother's closest cousin and friend. She also wondered what she would do after the money she saved was gone. She was concerned about that because the lion share of the money her mother had squirreled away disappeared with Skeeter and DC. There were only $5,000 left, and even though she was only around twenty-three years old, she clearly understood that this would not come close to lasting her throughout her life, nor would it be enough to finance the life of elegance she envisioned. So she felt the only thing left was to try and get a good-paying job and start from there. The next day, she started inquiring about possible employment opportunities. She started speaking with church members in hopes they could point her in the right direction. She was open to virtually any job as long as it was not outside or working in the field planting or harvesting crops. Her adamant position of not working in the fields was tied to her opinion about her beauty. After all, her entire life, people had remarked about how lovely she was and had complimented her lean, slender flawless body. She fancied that if she stayed away from the sunbaking fields, she could keep her looks longer, and that was of tremendous importance. She continued asking those she came in contact with for employment opportunities, not fully understanding that her greatest opportunity to work in that form would not be the work to which most black women yearned, and that was to work in the homes of affluent whites, cooking, cleaning, washing, and serving as babysitter for their children. But truthfully, for Dominique, it was a matter of work, pure and simple, as long as it was inside for the most part.

Within a few weeks, Dominique saw Ms. Margaret coming out of the store and assisted her with her bags. This was not very unusual at this time given the nature of the Deep South, but Dominique took this opportunity to ask Ms. Margaret concerning anybody looking for a housemaid. Ms. Margaret responded by shaking her head to symbolize no. So the ashamed Dominique said, "Thank you, Ms. Margaret. I'm sorry I bothered, you but how is Mr. Billy?"

Margaret said, "He's OK. Now could you just pick up the rest of my stuff, put it in the car, and go away? I ain't got nothing for you or your kind." Dominque said, "I'm sorry, Ms. Margaret. I meant no harm, ma'am." Margret said, "Huh?" and got in the car and drove down the road just a very short distance. She looked in the rearview mirror and saw Dominique staring at the car she drove seemingly in total disbelief. Dominique was obviously bewildered by Margaret's responses because she thought Margaret was fond of her as she had become of her. Abruptly, Margaret stopped the car and backed up to Dominique and said tearfully, "Dominique, I'm sorry. You are a fine girl. I was short with you because my mind was crowded with as many other things, and forgive me." Dominique replied, "Of course, Ms. Margaret, I understand a lady as important as you have many things to think about. I'm just sorry for asking you about work, seeing you ain't got time to be thinking about my little problems." Margaret said, "Oh no, child, that was just inconsiderate on my part. And if you want a job, you can come be my housekeeper starting first thing in the morning. Seeing how your ma was our housekeeper before she passed, it's only right that we offer you her job." Dominique said, "Do you mean that, Ms. Margaret?"

"Sure, child," said Margaret. "The job will be yours if you want it, and tomorrow, we will discuss your wages when you report to work. I'll expect you around seven in the morning and don't be late." Dominique said, "Madam, have no worry, I'll surely be there."

Starting a new job was very uplifting for Dominique. Her excitement was visible to all who saw her that day. When asked where she would be working, she enthusiastically told them it was for Ms. Margaret, and everybody told her that she was very fortunate to take over her mother's job. She felt the same, and the night before she was to begin her new job, she prayed and thanked God for the opportunity to work again. After praying so fervently, she anointed her head with oil and invoked the presence of God in her mind, body, and soul because she felt God was giving her another chance to build her life into an independent one. That night as she rested, her mind was consumed with the pleasant thoughts of having another chance. So excited was she that peaceful sleep never fully seemed to fall upon her. Instead, just before the breaking of day, she jumped out of the bed and began to dance and shout. In her mind, the job opportunity bore a striking resemblance to David in the Old Testament dancing before the Lord as he had moved the Ark of the Covenant back toward Jerusalem, the holy city of Israel. She was exuberant just having a steady place to go every day, making some money, and reevaluating herself as one who is employed. She considered herself not just employed, but feeling restored and back in the swing of things.

Margaret seemed to have forgotten about the past and was ready to let bygones be bygones. But her evening habit of reading the Bible brought more than just biblical enlightenment; she would not fail to revisit a special place in the Bible that were written by her own hand. This handwritten part was there wrapped tightly in the sacred book of antiquity. At the first notice of Dominique, it appeared to be just personal thoughts about special events regarding places they had visited and various comments that she valued. For example, there were comments from various episodes of her children growing up, from the time they learned to ride a bike to their Baptism day, etc. Dominique thought it was quite nice of Margaret to have a record of these special moments of her children. So Dominique never touched the book even when she was cleaning all around it. She considered bothering Ms. Margaret's Bible was to defame the very high regard to which it was written.

Dominique, possessing even greater skill than her mother to win people and for them to give up position in favor of hers, never asked to explore Margaret's Bible. She had decided to stay away from it even though the seemingly ordinary Bible with personal notes inserted did raise her curiosity. What she thought was so unusual was the way Margaret seemed to guard it. Dominique began to think that maybe there was a hidden secret that Margaret wanted to protect. Her thoughts about Margaret's unusual protection of the Bible were further heightened by her temper which exploded when Dominique was sweeping and accidentally struck the table's leg, and the Bible fell to the floor, and detached papers fell out on the floor. Margaret scolded Dominique and demanded that she became more careful when cleaning anywhere around her Bible. Dominique was apologetic and assured her that it would never happen again. And from this point, Dominique was very careful but certainly more curious about this particular Bible. There were other Bibles in the house that had no real significance to Margaret, but this one was almost worshipped. Although Dominique was not familiar with the theological term *bibliolatry*, it means the worship of the Bible is also considered sinful. All Dominique knew was there must be something in this particular Bible that had great value to Margaret, and Dominique became intrigued in finding out what it was.

While she was curious about Margaret's apparent secret, she was also dealing with what she considered a call into the ministry. So she expressed her interest in pursuing her call into the ministry to her pastor, and he started a series of meetings with her to assist her in preparation of fulfilling her mission in the ministry. Week after week, she would leave work and meet with her pastor to discuss the ministry. After weeks of meeting with her pastor, he noticed an attitude change in Dominique. He asked her if she was sure that this was what she wanted to do because once she goes in, there are no exit doors, but she assured him it was only some long days at work, and she was quite tired sometimes. The pastor was comforted by her response and proceeded to continue to teach her about the ministry.

But as she learned more about the ministry, her curiosity about Margaret's Bible continued to increase. She became obsessed with what was so special in that Bible. So the next day, she awoke with the idea that she would find out what was kept in it.

When Dominique arrived at work that day, seemingly from nowhere, DC showed up at her workplace, requesting to speak with her for just a quick moment. Margaret responded by suggesting to him that she was working and was not to receive any visitors while working. DC was kind and docile but requested that she let her know he went by and wanted her to call him later. He emphasized that it was rather important. Margaret was not very interested in whatever DC wanted and swiftly dismissed him. But Dominique, while gazing through the window, saw DC and thought it was rather odd that he would stop by to see her especially when she thought he was aware of her immensely negative feelings toward him and Skeeter. Her anger toward them was rooted in the fact that the money saved by her mother, Louise, disappeared when these two left. But his visit was still a matter of interest. In her mind, she tied his visit to her curiosity about Margaret's Bible. Somehow, she reasoned that her call into the ministry gave her special and unique access to the revelation of God. And consequently, she felt, DC's visit and Margaret's Bible were related in some way. She became more determined to find out what all these meant. At the close of the day, DC showed up again and found Dominique arriving home and expressed he wanted to talk to her. Dominique was not very inviting but asked him to talk to her. DC responded quickly by simply saying he believed the woman that she was working for knew something about Louise's death. Dominique wanted to know on what he was basing his information.

He said, "'Cuz that ol' bat found out about Billy helping Louise."

Dominique said, "Man, what you talkin' 'bout?"

DC said, "Listen, I got my information from the janitor from her church who heard her talking about it to another woman in the chapel. They did not know the janitor, my friend John, was just on the other side of the door, and that's all I was trying to tell you."

"OK," said Dominique, "I'll check it out."

Now Dominique developed a greater interest in reading the Bible Margaret cherished. Days and weeks passed, and Dominique continued to look for an opportunity to get to that Bible. And finally, Margaret reassumed a position of comfort about Dominique, left her at the house alone, and went to the hospital to visit a sick friend. Her Bible was in her bedroom in her nightstand with the bedroom door thought to be locked. But it was not. So Dominique took this opportunity to find out what was in it. After about an hour of searching, she found it and began to flip through the pages and notes that were written by her, and they were jaw-dropping. It wasn't long before she found notes like those in a personal diary. The notes revealed that Margaret planned, plotted, and executed the murder of Louise. Her mother's death was clearly fueled by jealously and the feeling of deceit. Margaret expressed a vehement hate for Louise and called her in the notes "the slick nigga whore." She continued to reveal just how vile she found Louise, and the true beauty she possessed reminded saved white decent folk of the ugliness of Satan. Her writing was graphic and nasty. She wrote about how it was her Christian duty to rid the community of people like Louise, and her murdering her did not disturb her any more than killing a gnat in an outhouse.

Dominique was livid after reading just how cold Margaret could be. She knew she could be unpleasant but had no idea she could be a cold-blooded murder. And as she thought about what Margaret did to her mother, she lit a flame of fire in her blood that what she did to the colonel years ago would seem like a walk in the park. Amid the lust for revenge she now felt, she also tried with all her might to contain her emotions. But that was not easy. Day after day, the thoughts of revenge continued to cascade across her mind. She would pray every night to seek divine help in exorcising the demons of anger that were assembled in her spirit. The pain and agony of her mother's death, along with the way she died, pierced her soul daily. She would begin to cry without any apparent reason, and those who saw her were never given any explanation. Her struggle with confusion was kept hidden in her heart because she felt alone. Besides, she figured, who could she tell? She understood she was a black girl from the poorest section in town. She had no real friends since her mother was gone, and nobody would believe her story. And if they did, there was nothing that anyone could do. This was the Deep South, and she knew the law was not an ally to blacks. Besides, she also felt the hedge trimmer incident that led to the murder of the colonel, to which she was the culprit, fostered the idea that it is probably best to leave the law out of it. Dominique now found herself angry and totally confused but felt like she needed to do something because this was about her mother, the only one that really loved her.

The next week, she met with her pastor for their weekly meeting. She tried to be upbeat but was not her bubbly self. But she tried to remain attentive and take in the learning for the day, however she was visibly troubled. Her pastor tried to probe into her spirit by inquiring if anything was wrong with her. But she never opened up to share her feelings or concerns and would hastily redirect the conversation back to ministerial matters. The pastor continued to press Dominique to allow him to help her, but over and over again, she would not take the opportunity. She just wanted him to pray for her without ceasing, citing the Bible, "The prayers of the righteous availeth much." She assured her pastor that while she was dealing with many issues, she was really OK and just wanted to get prepared for her initial sermon. Although, deep in her heart, she wanted to talk to her pastor about what was troubling her, she thought there was nothing he could do that would make any measurable difference. However, she did recognize that if she didn't address this with somebody, her anger might get the best of her and cause her to be in legal trouble.

Since she was not comfortable in speaking with her pastor about her discovery, she went home wishing someone could help her. The next day, as she went to work, she was praying most of the way when Burnie saw her coming past the drugstore, and he ran up to her and spoke. He seemed delighted to see her and remarked how pretty she was. He couldn't seem to ignore her striking resemblance to her mother. It just took him back to the pleasant days of his meetings with Louise. He was tearing up as he discussed Louise with Dominique. So emotional was he that he apologized to Dominique as he took his handkerchief to wipe the tears that started falling down from his eyes onto his visibly red face. As he became more composed, Dominique asked if she could speak to him privately about a matter very close to her heart. Burnie assured her he would gladly help her in any way he could. He wanted her to know her mother was a great lady that he respected and admired. He did not, however, mention in any way that she was his paramour and that he would protect her always. But Dominique's serious tone led him to believe that perhaps she was going to ask him about her mother's personal interactions. He braced himself for having to possibly explain something of a sexual nature she may have accidently seen during one of the late pleasure parties he had had with Louise. He feared questions about his deceased lover and the mother of her now-mature daughter. His fear was heightened by the known realities about his own life, namely, he was married, and he had been married for decades. He was a city councilman of multiple terms and an avid church attendee. He was considered a strong Christian despite his apparent business success. In preparation of Dominique's inquisition, he asked her, "Does this have anything to do with your mother?"

She replied, "Sorta, but it has more to do with Ms. Margaret."

Burnie almost revealed a sigh of relief. He asked her to please proceed and let him know how he could help her.

She said, "Mr. Burnie, I know how my mother died and who killed her."

Burnie said, "What do you mean? I was told she had some type of attack that had something to do with her blood and brain."

"No, sir," said Dominique.

Burnie said, "But how, who, what happened?"

Dominique started tearing up. anger became visible in her face, and her body started to tremble. Burnie hugged her to comfort her and said, "It's all right, darling, just calm down," as he patted her on her back and shoulders. He then said, "Please tell me what happened."

Dominique said, "It was Ms. Margaret, the heifer I worked for. I read it in her Bible. She kept the notes of how she was going to kill my mama cuz she thought Mr. Billy was seeing my mama late on Tuesday nights, and my mama working in her house like nothing was going on, and it makes her so jealous she killed her, Mr. Burnie. That woman killed my mama." Burnie was enraged. While trying to comfort Dominique, he was really mad. His anger was based on a few things all at the same time. First of all, Louise was his heart. He really loved her and did not believe anything was ever going on with her and Billy. Secondly, on Tuesday nights, he was with Louise. That was their night together, and he never missed one. Thirdly, he missed Louise so much, he felt lonely and isolated without her. And looking at Dominique's face crying in pain brought back the image of his most loved woman, Louise, back in full display. He too was in pain.

The next day, Dominique found the strength to deal with the task of work. This day, she had a better handle on her work, with a better attitude toward Ms. Margaret. As she cleaned and cooked that day, she began to hum and smile. Margaret inquired about her very happy demeanor, and Dominique just inferred she spent the night in serious prayer. She continued to share how prayer will ultimately help one to be focused and determined, and this, she said, would lead one to unspeakable joy. Margaret was very happy to hear about her apparent newly found joy. Margaret said, "Since you have done such a wonderful job today already, you can get off a whole hour early if you like."

Dominique said, "I sure do, and thank you for your kindness, Ms. Margaret."

"You're welcome Dominique," Margaret said.

At the appointed hour, Dominique gathered her things and headed toward the door and said, "Good evening, Ms. Margaret."

Margaret said harshly, "Where do you think you are going? It's not time for you to go, so you get yourself back in that kitchen."

Dominique said, "But, Ms. Margaret, I thought you told me I could leave an hour earlier today?"

Margaret said, "Are you crazy, girl? I said no such thing. Now get back in that kitchen."

Dominique's rage and anger seemed to be on their way back in the residence of her soul. She felt like this woman lied to her today. After finding this woman killed her mama, "I should take this knife and stick it deep it in her chest," were the thoughts of Dominique. But then a spirit of peace calmed her down enough to think about the ministry she was about to enter. When she worked the last hour and was about to leave, Billy entered the house and spoke to Dominique. She spoke back and bid him goodbye at the same time. Then Billy asked if he could see her out front for just a minute. She obliged and wanted to know if her work was satisfactory. He assured her that her work was wonderful, and he had absolutely no complaints. He wanted her to know that the reason he wanted to speak to her was to inform her that Ms. Margaret was in the early stages of Alzheimer's, and sometimes she gets confused or does not remember things well at all. Dominique was thankful to Billy for the information because it helped her understand the mood swings. So she left that day feeling better about things at work, inasmuch as Billy provided her assurance of his satisfaction in her work.

Dominique prepared to go to her weekly meeting with her pastor as she was approaching the Sunday of her initial sermon, and she wanted things to be special for all who would be assembled to hear her present the Word of God. So this was the day when the pastor would provide her with sermon structure and textual interpretation. She was very excited about going home and putting some of what she had learned to work. The pastor saw her face light up with great enthusiasm and told her she would be a fine minister. He told her she would be a blessing to all who hears her preach, but that's why he has become sadder and sadder to have to tell her what he believed she needed to know. Dominique was anxious to know what the pastor was talking about, so she asked him.

The pastor said," Dominique, there is no other way to say this, but last night, I met with my deacons, and they unanimously voted to not permit you to preach here." Dominique was crushed, and she asked why.

The pastor responded, "Their reasons were number 1, you are a woman, and they don't believe in female ministers. Second, one of the officers shared an experience he had with your mother regarding his house, and it was most unpleasant."

"But, Pastor, that has nothing to do with me," Dominique said.

He replied, "You are so right, dear, but what else can I do?"

"Well, you could be a man and stand up to those weak men!" she said. "Never mind, Pastor. I'll confront them myself. Don't you worry. I got this!"

The pastor said, "OK, sweetheart. I hope it all works out for you."

The next evening was prayer meeting and Bible study, and Dominique was there. She sang a beautiful song and inserted her popular sermonic material in her presentation and shared how the enemy has been trying to keep her from preaching the Word and using the leaders in the church to do it. The church stood in powerful opposition to anyone impeding Dominique's desire to preach. Besides, as most of them mentioned, she would be the first female to begin a ministry from there and by far the best one. The members in large numbers threatened to leave the church and start another one. It became quite testy, and the pastor called an emergency meeting with his officers that very night in an attempt to get control of the whole matter. They quickly voted again and immediately offered an apology to Dominique. They insisted with humility that she deliver her initial sermon as soon as she and the pastor could arrange it.

She thanked them and said, "Pastor and I will work things out, and giving God praise and glory is all we were trying to do."

"Thank you, and God bless you," said Deacon Mac, the chairman.

Dominique left and went home. The church seemed very excited about her preaching, and she immersed herself in deep study. She immediately pulled out her books, Bibles, and commentaries and began to read them. As she shut herself in the private room of her house, she had a visitor at the door. She went to the door, and it was Burnie. He was trembling and crying. Dominique insisted that he come so she could help him. He was out of control and couldn't seem to gather himself to talk to her. So she continued to try to console him, but at this time, nothing seemed to work. She offered him something to drink, and he took it and started to calm himself. She then more aggressively inquired about what was troubling him. Dominique's curiosity had surely piqued, and she felt that she really needed to know what was troubling him. He started speaking very slowly, pausing frequently, because he was still somewhat emotional. He started telling her that he had made a terrible mistake, so Dominique urged him to continue. Burnie explained that his mistakes had to do with Ms. Margaret. Dominique was perplexed at that statement because she couldn't imagine what this was about. But Burnie continued his story by sharing the fact that he had just visited the house of Margaret, and she was alone. He told her she knew that Billy was not home because it was prayer meeting night, and Billy always attended the service. He told Dominique that when he got there, Margaret was upstairs in her sewing room, mending a few things. He tried again to fight back his tears but managed to tell Dominique that when she answered the door and let him in, she said, "Billy is not here, but he'll be here soon. If you like to wait, you can sit in the living room, and I'll join you shortly. I need to tidy up my sewing room."

Then Burnie told Dominique that she went upstairs, and he pretended to go to the living room. But instead, he waited until she was out of sight and slipped up the stairs and confronted her about the killing of Louise.

Margaret became angry, saying, "How dare you confront me about killing anyone, especially that whorish Louise?"

Burnie continued and said, "When she said that, something snapped in me, and my love for Louise caused me to grab her. I wanted to choke her, but then I caught myself and just pushed her very hard. We were standing near the stairs, and as I pushed her, she stumbled backward and fell down the stairs. I didn't know what to do, so I ran as fast as I could down the stairs, and she was not breathing. I began to panic, so I went to her bedroom looking for the Bible you mentioned to me to get it so no one would ever see what you saw." Dominique began to cry because although she had harbored bad feelings about Margaret, she didn't want her killed, unless she had the opportunity to do it. She especially did not want her dead in light of what Billy told her about Margaret being in the early stages of Alzheimer's. Dominique, after wiping tears from her eyes, asked Burnie if he got the Bible.

Burnie said, "I got it in my car." He then went to get it, and they both went through all the pages. After going through the pages, they found out that the Thursday nights she thought Billy was seeing Louise were actually Tuesday nights when Burnie was there. And Margaret's rage and jealously toward Louise were based on her thinking that Billy was with her on Tuesday nights, but it was Burnie all the time.

Dominique's response was, "Mr. Billy, you shouldn't have done that because Ms. Margaret's mind has been leaving her for quite some time. Mr. Billy told me so just the other day. Really, I am not sure if anything is true or not because her mind was not well.

"Oh my god," said Burnie, and he continued to tell Dominique that he has been in love with Louise for many years.

"Of course we tried to keep it a secret because we knew no one would understand. I really love her, Dominique, and I am sorry to tell you all of this," said Burnie.

Dominique said, "It's done now, Mr. Burnie."

Burnie said, "Of course this has to remain between us the rest of our lives.

Dominique, it's way too ugly, and too much would have to come out, and we shouldn't have your mother's memory besmirched by an ugly scandal."

Dominique said, "Ugly or not, I am preparing to go into ministry, and my conscience will not allow me to participate in this murder. We have to call the police because a crime has been committed."

Burnie said, "Since when did your conscience become so big? Where was your conscience when you took the hedge trimmers pretending to pleasure the colonel, and you castrated him and left him to bleed to death? Oh yes, I know about that story, and your mother did too! So I kept your secret for all these years, and I expect you to keep mine!" Dominique was ashamed and became very emotional.

He asked her, "So we have a deal?"

Fighting tears and trying to gather herself, she uncontrollably nodded yes. He said, "Are you sure?" She answered, "Yes, I understand we have a deal." Dominique was visibly upset but managed to pull herself together to fully understand the covenant she had just made with Burnie.

While she was dealing with these matters of the heart and conscience, the time was quickly approaching when she would publicly declare her call into the ministry. She was actually down to her last meeting with the pastor before she would embark on the intricate journey of preaching the Gospel. So she walked into the pastor's office and sat comfortably in the chair and said, "Pastor, I'm ready." She presented her sermon to the pastor and waited for him to respond. After the pastor's critique of her message, she aptly gathered her belongings and headed home. She seemed to have one thing occupying her mind, and that was in a couple of weeks, she would be sharing the Gospel with her church members. So she thought the best thing to do now was pray and seek divine guidance on how she would present the message she finally believed the Lord had given her. As she knelt to pray, she heard a knock at the door. She didn't want to answer but decided to answer and dismiss the visitor quickly. Little did she know, it was Burnie again. He spoke and quickly got into the reason of his visit. He wanted to know if she was all right and if she remembered the covenant the two of them had made. She became annoyed by his presence and began to shout obscenities at him. She then recollected herself, rather quickly, apologized, and asked him to leave. His feelings were hurt, and tearfully, he assured her he meant no harm. The real reason for the visit was to tell her that Margaret's funeral was scheduled for the early part of the week and wanted her to know it in case she wanted to go. Dominique assured him she was not interested in going, and her energy was only focused on her initial sermon. She also told him that she dreaded going to work and was already planning to move once her ministry had begun. Burnie left and said, "Good night and God bless you." Dominique responded in kind and said,

"I hope you can make it to my initial sermon service." Burnie said, "I have been hearing about that and would not miss it for the world." Dominique smiled and waved goodbye. But she noticed Burnie was moving very slowly, almost dragging himself to the car. So she asked him, "Are you OK?" He said, "I think so, but my energy has been very low, and my appetite has not been good. But I'll be all right. I'll stop by the doctor sometime, but do have a good night." She said, "You too."

As Burnie drove home, Dominique realized two things about herself that had not been apparent earlier. First of all, she came to realize that she had a quick temper; and second, it dawned on her that she did care about the well-being of Burnie. Perhaps, her concern about Burnie was rooted in the fact that now she clearly knew about the illicit affair he had with her mother. Along with the latter realization, she could feel the genuine love he had for her mother. Although she understood their relationship was filled with salacious, lewd activity, her love for her mother was unshaken. She loved her mother, and whatever her mother did was done to make a better life for herself and her children. But her concern for Burnie was something she knew would not be easy to shake because he was her mother's sponsor in many things. So she got back on her knee and began to pray for strength, wisdom, and direction as she begins her ministry for God. By the time she finished praying, her heart seemed still heavy about the health of Burnie, but she convinced herself it was probably nothing and went to sleep. But it was more than nothing. The next day, she learned that Burnie had a stroke, and paralysis had set in on him. The news saddened her deeply, and the entire day, her thoughts seemed to meander back to whom she considered a friend, Mr. Burnie. She learned he was trying to fight through it, but it was believed the stroke caused permanent damage, and he would remain in a wheelchair for the rest of his life and never to walk again.

While she dealt with the pain of Burnie's condition, she also knew that the time of her initial sermon was near. So she studied and prayed much to ensure that she would to be prepared for her ministerial moment. Dominique withdrew herself from many of the usual duties for a period of fasting and purification. Each morning, she would anoint herself and then meditate in an attempt to invoke the presence of God in her daily walk. She seemed immersed in this exercise because she truly believed it was the will of God for her to be the catalyst behind a new concept in ministry. As she prayed, she was always cognizant of the unmistakable realities associated with her ministry. The fact that she was a female was certainly something she could not change, but the question in her mind regarding her gender was, would people really take her seriously? Also, she was a very beautiful woman. And since traditional churches consisted of more women than men, how would she realistically have a consistent audience? She knew that the chemistry existing between a black male pastor and a black female parishioner was almost sacred in and of itself, and nothing she felt would ever rival that. Then she considered the type of ministry to which she had been called. In her mind, the ministry of tradition was not what she felt God had called her. There was a new idea of ministry that appealed to her although she had really never seen it. The Gospel that prepared people to die (what theologians call the Doctrine of Eschatology) was the popular Gospel espoused by every minister and pastor in the region and era. But as she prepared to preach, she sought to deliver a different idea of God, one she considered fresh and new. She was not sure what it was or how it would even be received, but she felt she would know it when she either heard it or saw it.

As days went by, as she was continuing her search in the type of ministry she would promote, it was almost by accident, but she would insist it was by divine design, that she opened the Bible one day, and the book opened to Ecclesiastes 10:19. Unaware that this was her mother's favorite verse, she read the (B) part of the verse which suggested that money was the answer to all things. When she thought about the verse, she concluded that this verse would serve as the foundation of her ministry. This also, she felt, would appeal to a wide black audience because at this time in the Deep South, the lack of money seemed to be the denominator that all blacks had in common. So she immediately began putting her thoughts and ideas together on paper but struggled to come up with a name for the concept. She knew it could not appear to be a ministry blatantly calling for money but felt like it needed a name for the concept that would appear to be aligned with the will of God. Her idea of ministry was one where she needed to be the author or leader of a spiritual cultural shift in the black religious experience. She continued to think about the name of the concept. One must remember, she had no formal theological training whatsoever, but let's understand that at this time, that was not a requirement for ministry in the black community. Her goal was to have a name for the concept that would validate her initial sermonic presentation. The sermon was going to be about money for sure, but a catchy name would nurture justification for her sermon's content. At last, she came up with a name for the concept, the Prosperity Gospel. "Wow!" she fancied. "That's it! That name captures what I plan to offer the people who hear me."

The Prosperity Gospel is the Gospel that produces money for you if you invest your money in making the man or woman of God rich. It was that simple. By sewing money into the man or woman of God, God would shower you with riches, good health, good relationships, etc. And if you are not reaping great harvests from giving to them, you need to give more. The Prosperity Gospel had not been shared with blacks in the Deep South, and the thought of her being the first to preach and teach it brought a profound sense of importance to young Dominique. Relevance and personal importance were necessary to her because she had wooed churches with her incredibly singing talent but thought teaching them about making money by praising God. The idea of this kind of ministry, she believed, would work well for her because after all, just like her wonderfully singing mother, getting paid outweighed everything else. This, she thought, would immediately secure an audience. Her preparation was quite methodical. She searched the Bible carefully to find as many scriptures as she could and developed them into a very convincing message of existential wealth through giving to the pulpiteers. She also believed, if she could sell this concept, it would allow her the financial wherewithal to care for those who seemed to struggle in making their ends meet. This, she considered, would put her in a position of power with the people, which would further raise her social importance and significance. It was really amazing that a very young soon-to-be minister had already determined the type of ministry she would develop and promote.

Well, the Sunday for the scheduled date of her initial sermon had finally come. The exact time was three o'clock in the afternoon. The weather was a balmy sunny day with intermittent breezes that provided a wonderful refreshing atmosphere. It was well anticipated, and the community at large all seemed to be there. The cars were shining, people were immaculately dressed, and smiles of joy and expressions of curiosity were all present to witness this young female enter the ministry. And of course, this event was monumental for the community because it had not been done before. So there everybody was, looking to see whether this would be a success, or it would simply be a mockery of God. Among the anxious attendees was a surprise visitor named Mr. Charles Burnhart, known to Dominique as Burnie. She had not seen him since the stroke, and although he was in a wheelchair, he was ecstatic to see her. She too was happy to see him but visibly saddened by his condition. The pastor called the service to order, and it started energetically as anticipated. The choir was in rare form as their mellifluous voices filled the sanctuary. Members, friends, and visitors alike frequently stood throughout the service, clapping their hands, stomping their feet, shouting, and dancing as the melodies and prayers were presented. Finally, the pastor stood to introduce this singing sensation and announce formally that Dominique, with a burning in her heart for God, would publicly present the Word of God today to officially enter the ranks of the ecclesiastical order, the professional sacred call, and the ministry of God. By the time he mentioned the last portion of his rather magniloquent introduction, the entire assembly rose to their feet and gave her a standing ovation. And from that reception, Dominique felt "it was on."

The moment had finally come when she would publicly assert her call into the ministry. So she stood with her head lowered in reverent humility, saying nothing, while the excited congregants praised God loudly. But she continued to stand, wearing a dark pant suit with a hint of pink pinstripe. Her custom-made suit draped over a soft pink blouse with an open collar that slightly revealed a gold chain around her neck. For shoes, she wore dark pumps that complemented her classy outfit. Her nails were beautifully manicured with a soft pink polish that highlighted her acute attention to detail. To complete her stunning attire was her soft long naturally fine hair that fell past her shoulders, and many were astonished and spellbound by its length. Her makeup seemed to have been done by a Hollywood cosmetologist. It was faint and light but done to perfection to just accentuate the natural beauty to which she was endowed. Oh my, it seemed like a movie star was in the house. After the applauses and cheers, Dominique, with the poise of a twenty-five-year veteran, began to speak. She recognized protocol and prepared the friendly crowd for her message by singing a solo, for which she had become known. It was "Precious Lord, Take My Hand." Her beautifully polished voice demonstrated such range and jazzy slurs characteristic of both the Black Jazz and Gospel Era, and everybody seemed emotionally taken by her rendition. By now, the crowd was ready and pumped for the Word she would deliver.

But this message would not simply fall into the category of popular black preaching. During this time, as alluded to earlier, the message espoused by the typical black preacher was one that nurtured hope that was to come in an afterlife relationship. The change was not in your personal condition, but rather in your exit from earthly experiences. And many blacks of the era embraced this idea because there were no signs in this life that life could be anything other than the life of struggle to which the masses had become accustomed. The expected message from her was one that would have been filled with eschatological, or better stated "after death," images and symbols. For example, "you got shoes, and I got shoes and all God chulluns got shoes, and when we get to heaven, we gonna put on our shoes and shout all over God's heaven." Other symbols such as wings, robes, golden streets, and mansions were a part of the theological understanding of the era. But Dominique, well aware of the social and spiritual understanding of popular preaching embarked on another theological discourse. She brought into the consciousness of the congregants that God wants them to be prosperous, rich, and sitting at the head table rather than being stuck or satisfied with just serving those seated there. It was radical, she was radical, her outfit was radical, and she appeared quite comfortable shaking things up. She wanted them to know God called her to be radical, and it's time for everybody to take back what the devil stole from them. Wow! The congregation seemed to say. She had the congregation begging for more.

Discouraged, sometimes I am when I recognize the absurdity in trying to be perfect, but the call to excellence is so obsessive it persuades me to go after it.

–J. Gentile Everett

They loved what they were hearing. It was fresh and alluring because she pointed out how fatigued the poor community was and shouted, "We've been down so long, it looks like up to us." The screaming, shouting crowd seemed to have reached a fever pitch, yelling, hollering, and falling out, and many seemed caught up in eternal dances. The organ played to the rhythm of each word she spoke, and the congregation would moan melodiously in response to her instruction. The call-and-response motif indicative of the church was in full display. Amid all their spiritual and emotional pandemonium, Brother Burnie managed to roll his wheelchair closer to the altar, with obvious tears flowing from his eyes. He was able to raise his hand in what appeared as sincere praise, and then he jerked in his chair and dropped his head in death. It appeared Burnie had a heart attack from seeing Dominique capture a crowd's attention the same way her mother, Louise, captured his heart.

He was rolled out of the church, and the ambulance arrived very quickly at the church, but it was too late. Burnie had lived to see the daughter of his all-time lover become a woman, and he had strongly believed she was way too gifted to ever be compared with the ordinary. The worship service continued, but Dominique paused just before she ended her message for the church to pray for Burnie and his family. That day as truly an eventful one with much drama, but Dominique left the church with $2,000 from the congregation, which was an unheard of amount. This honorarium supported her theology that preaching a gospel of prosperity obviously works. And this was further substantiated in her mind the next day when Dominique was given a check from Burnie for $5,000 that had been found in his jacket pocket the day he passed. She was quite happy at how everything went that day with the exception of Burnie's death.

The other side of her intricate personality, however, was somewhat relieved at his death. Dominique was always concerned about her life over and above all else. One of her concerns was how long could or would Burnie have kept her dark secret. As long as he lived, she thought, she would remain under the threat of his revealing what he knew about the colonel's death. He was the only one who had ever mentioned anything to her about it. She had always wanted some way of controlling what Burnie might say about it at some later time, and the information regarding her murdering Margaret to avenge Margaret's crime against Louise would not really amount to much because of the political and social climate of the era. Regardless of her popularity, she understood she was black, and there was nothing she could do to rise above the word of a rich white southern man. But now that he is dead, she could take comfort in believing everything was all right now. The secret would be buried with Burnie's body. The other issue that she thought was satisfied by his death was the way she felt about Burnie's private affair with her mother. She never told him, but she totally detested their relationship. She was convinced that Burnie did not love Louise but simply used his power over her to lure her into a sleazy affair of sex and exploitation. Even after she got the $5,000 check after she preached her initial sermon, her heart was not changed. She interpreted the gift simply as an old sick man trying to ease his guilt-ridden conscience. Because once she found out what he was doing with Louise, she could only put it in the framework of how she felt when the murdered colonel used her simply as a new toilet to dispose of his semen nurtured by an old lust. And finally, she put into perspective the death of her mother, which was the reason Burnie was grief stricken. By losing Louise, he could no longer have his chocolate cake and vanilla ice cream.

The tide of ministry was changing now in Dominique's life. Her popularity and the demand for her service were increasing rapidly. She started to hang around with other ministers and pastors. The reception of her presence was usually pretty good. The ministry in the area was led by men only, and Dominique's presence, though largely welcomed, was met often with resentment and jealousy from other females. She managed to handle it rather well but always focused on what she was trying to do. Somewhere in her past, she developed a strong sense of determination, and this special quality would serve her well as she became more immersed in the ministry. The more she preached, the more others wanted her to preach. Her growing social and ministerial importance continued to rise in the community. So much so that there also was a growing sense of anger among ministers who were never able to garner that kind of recognition. Many of her haters would disseminate poisonous verbal attacks about her dressing standards and her involvements in what many considered sinful elements of the community, and sometimes, they were about her sexual orientation, hinting that maybe she was involved in a lesbian relationship with somebody. She was not yet ordained, and many ministers who sat on the ordination council vowed they would never vote for her to be ordained, regardless of her test scores, recommendations, or political pressure. Ordination was needed for her to ultimately be considered a leader and an approved and accepted professional minister. And although the challenge was surely going to come, she remained focused on a larger mission, and that was to rise above all those who were against her. Her pastor kept pushing her despite much opposition from her fellow clergymen, but she would constantly assure him it was OK whatever tide rose against her because in the end, her message and method of ministry would rise above their messages of theological backwardness that transports the Christians as wreckage to be piled up on poverty's junkyard.

After two years of seeking ordination, she found out that she did not necessarily have to be ordained by the local assembly of ministers. When she understood that her pastor and two other ordained ministers with the support of the church could ordain her, thus endowing her with all the rights and privileges of the clergy, she became more interested in her pastor leading the way to this end.

Pastor Wilson loved Dominique and was excited about her ministry. However, he was rather hesitant in becoming involved in participating in this unconventional method to ordination. Yes, it was legal, but Pastor Wilson felt such a bold move would undermine his credibility in the ministerial alliance. Also, Dominique had no criminal record. There were those in the community who simply thought there was simply something strange about her. The pastor understood well how explosive this issue was, and because of the political cost of such a move, he decided not to pursue it. Dominique got word that Pastor Wilson was not interested in providing leadership and assisting her with her ordination. She met with him to discuss his position. Surely enough, Pastor Wilson acknowledged that although he did not know what to do, he was at least clear that he could not risk his standing in the ministerial alliance for her and this ordination thing. Dominique was not shaken by his position; in fact, she anticipated it. So when the pastor finished presenting his position, Dominique presented hers. She wanted the pastor to know that she never wanted to share her information with him but felt obligated now. The pastor said, "What information are you talking about?" She said, "Well, two years ago, you went to a national convention in Nashville, Tennessee, along with three other pastors. One of the pastors expressed interest in a prostitute. The pastor said, "What does that have to do with me?" "Well," she said, "the same ministers had you in the car when somehow found a pimp named Cross Country and told him he was looking for some 'snow.'" Snow was his reference to securing a white prostitute for a night of pleasure. "And after your ministry friend was finished with her, he pimped her to many of your friends who were staying there and you knew it."

"Dominique, dear, I have no control over what other people do," the pastor said. He was quite shocked that she would ever come to him like that and became offended by her. He was becoming angry and uneasy. His anger had become quite obvious by the expressions on his face and insisted that she leave his office. But she said, "I was not finished telling you my story. The other part of my story involves you and your private companion for the convention. I know your brother picked up a Ms. Robinson, the lady who works in the association, so you could have private companionship while you were away. And the church gave you expense money for the trip, and you used a substantial portion entertaining your private guest. Also, you should know the reason I know all this is because I was there with a friend who hung out with your 'friend' every day. You see, one of the problems with senior citizen men is when they get a young, pretty girl that they think likes them, they usually drain your pockets dry, make you old dudes think y'all still got it, pretend like they are really into you, spend your money on some young dude, and come back for more when it runs out. And they usually get it. All it takes is tight pants, heels, a pitiful story for you old dudes, and for you to be allowed to pat them on their butt, and you guys will give them what they want every time." Pastor Wilson said, "You are a sick young lady in need of great help. What's the matter with you?" Dominique was not bothered by the pastor's anger. But in the end, she became ordained, and that was all she needed to establish her own ministry.

Dominique constantly reminded herself that she would do whatever it took to make it to the top. She would be at the top of her game. She would be the one that everyone, male or female, desired to be. Dominique often reflected on her early years of life before she observed the underhanded, unorthodox ways of successful men and her mother. She observed that those who acquired the most cared the least about those individuals who were affected or got in the way. She noticed that the ones who stayed quiet or were legate were never successful and were left to live a life of servitude and uncertainty and live in a cyclical silo of want. She knew that before the age of nine or so, she wanted to do the right thing. She wanted to make it the right way. But then reality set into her psyche.

She began to see that her life would take a different path. Her mother had demonstrated this all her young life. She learned right away that selling your heart, mind, body, and spirit could be bought in many ways without even coins exchanging hands. The cost was mere survival, survival in a male-dominated society where there was only minimal space in the barrel for that one female to get out. Instead, the price for true happiness could be paid with alcohol, drugs, sex, and more importantly, a deep, dark mind that would take her to places she thought she could have never imagined. Dominique was strengthened by this revelation, for this revelation meant that she would never be caught in the lifelong trap of trying to get what she wanted the right way. A lifelong battle of fighting legitimately was a toss-up. It could or could not pay off in the end, and that was a chance that Dominique was not willing to take.

Dominique was willing to take that chance on the dark side. She quickly snapped out of her thoughts of legitimacy and transplanted herself back to the here and now. She knew that she had to come up with a scheme that would propel her to the top of the ministerial game, a game where saving souls was secondary and securing their bodies for herself was primary. What could she do next? She knew that she could win over the male mind, but winning over female parishioners would be another story. But she needed them too if she were to continue to build her empire in this world. But it was just at that moment, on a Saturday night, that she realized how and when she would do it.

Following her ordination, she felt she was now qualified to take on the responsibilities of a pastorate. She had heard that the Star Community Church in a nearby city was without a leader. She also had been told the contact name for an appointment to speak was Deacon Bennie. She contacted the deacon, and they established a date for her to come and speak to their church. She prepared herself assiduously because she wanted to make an indelible impression upon all who heard her.

"I have to be smart," Dominique reminded herself as she reflected on the plan she lay awake in bed thinking about the night before. "Today, I am going to present this congregation with a message they have never heard of before in their lives." Dominique found herself preaching at a time that was a turning point in black society. The Old Time Way was starting to wane, and a younger generation of men and women was trying to figure out how to become as successful without a lot of hard work. Dominique clearly understood that at this point in her life, there were a few things that made the world go round, including money and, of course, the female population. In her mind, every underhanded deal, every illegal transaction, and every aspect of success involved women in some form or fashion. Dominique knew that if she could get this message across to these young women, it would be key to her continuing to build her empire and recruit foot soldiers to tread the paths of the underbelly of her success.

The day for her to speak at Star Community Church was a special day, and it was blessed by a beautiful, balmy weather. On Sundays, Dominique always dressed to the nines in her Sunday best. She would always combine glamor and comfort, a feat that many, if not most of her parishioners, were not and would never be able to do. Dominique always donned gloves. Her hands were the only part of her body that she did not mind keeping covered. She thought that gloves were the epitome of excellence, especially white gloves. To her, they were an illusion for purity in the sight of others. Her gloves, no matter the color, would always match her outfit. She had them pulled just below her elbow.

She took special care to accessorize her outfit. She loved furs and had a different fur for each Sunday of the month. No fur was imitation. No animal was off-limits. To her, fur was the definition of elegance. Her dresses were always bright and colorful. Anyone that wore bright colors on a Sunday exuded confidence, especially women. She believed that her presentation was just as important as what she preached. Besides, she was trying to sell herself, which came at any price, and she was trying to sell her sermons which would bring souls by the hundreds to the sanctuary and to her own cause.

Dominique's hair was long and curly, and she was careful to make sure every strand was in place. She didn't have to use any pomade. She always questioned who her father may have been, as her features were nothing like her mother's round, flat features. Perhaps a man whom her mother owed a favor or a soldier passing through that had a ration card or privileges at the military commissary, probably Native American or Caucasian. Nevertheless, she was thankful for her long locks that flowed down her back, and she knew men longed to twirl and twist them as they fantasized about her as she threw her hair while she delivered the Word, so wearing a hat was always out of the question.

Because of the heat, Dominique did not wear panty hose, even though they were becoming more popular. Instead, she preferred to show her bare legs that were toned, yet feminine and shapely. She did, however, take the time to take a dark pencil and draw a straight line from her thighs to her ankles to give the illusion that she had on a hose, as the elderly women of the church were quick to frown upon bear legs in church. Dominique was meticulous about her wardrobe since she learned the importance of personal presentation. As an accent to her trademark legs, Dominique wore a slim-cut dress with bulging shoulder pads to bring attention to her shapely hips, twenty-four-inch waist, and swanlike neck. Her shoes were equally as stunning. It was always a last-minute decision for her if she was going to wear her peep-toe wedges or her T-strap square heels. Her mind would always lead her to the right decision, and she was always a winner. Dominique depended lot on her inner voice, and never second guessed the advice that would come from within. That inner voice hadn't let her down with the wealth she had amassed so far, so surely, it wouldn't let her down when it came to picking out the appropriate shoes for the occasion.

Because Dominique was blessed with a natural physique which needed no artificial means of accentuation, she found it unnecessary to wear the typical garter and girdle since the panty hose were totally out of the question. She prided herself in being able to pull off the au naturel look with no assistance from bulky undergarments. A lack of underwear made her feel more feminine and, more importantly, allowed her to remind herself of what the real reason was for her being in the pulpit in the first place. A lack of underwear separated her from the rest of the women whom, for whatever reason, could not take the time to care for their bodies as they should. Her natural look reminded her that she had an edge over all the other women. She never had to toil in the fields because of acing the paper bag test with flying colors or have a litter of children from sweaty men as many of her parishioners had done, which imminently took a toll on many of their physical temples.

As night falls . . .

Dominique's last touch to her masterpiece was to make sure that her face was a canvas that all would remember that day and throughout the night in the dreams of men and women alike. She made sure that her eyebrows were thick and dark yet neatly arched and brushed. She applied mascara and eyeliner only to the top of her eye, just in case she had to cry for effect from a lined hymn or reverent prayer led by an old deacon that was past his time and prime. Here lips were perfectly lined and encased with a bright, fire engine red or coral pink lipstick that she applied to her lips with the sole intention of leaving her mark on everyone, male and female, that she kissed. She made sure that she filled in her lip stick beyond her natural lip line so that her full lips would seem fuller and more tantalizing than they actually were. As a singer, she would always sing a moving solo before she preached, and she knew that all the attention would be on her mouth and what was coming out of it. Oh yes, she felt she was ready for the stage now. Her costume was elaborate. In her mind, her presentation and entrance would be dramatic, a kind of drama where everyone would want a piece of her mind and body. She likened herself to Jesus Christ wearing a robe with tassels that the poor woman with the issue of blood felt the need to touch. And in Dominique's mind, she was a god about to walk through the city and perform miracles that would be etched in the malleable minds of the missionaries forever.

Dominique was ready to take the pulpit in which she now referred to as her stage. The congregation was full, packed to capacity even for a hot, sweltering July day. And as usual, the congregation was filled with three-fourth women and one-fourth men. She had already had her way with just about every male in the congregation in some form or fashion, so her focus on the female members was very timely. Dominique would always make her entrance about halfway through the service. That would give the congregation time to let their imaginations run wild with what they would anticipate she would have on for the day and what message she would dazzle them with. Dominique loved this. She loved this more than anything, with the exception of money being the center of attention, especially since it took her hours to prepare her overall look each Sunday.

Dominique always let other members of the pulpit make their entrance before her, ensuring that not one distraction would take away from her own personal entrance. A lot was at stake. She was going to deliver a message that had never been delivered in any congregation in the South or perhaps even in the United States. She was ready. She had reviewed this message, this plan, over and over in her mind. Not even her inner self spoke aloud about it. One misplaced word could thwart her whole plan in winning over the female congregation, and she couldn't afford that. As the choir began to sing and the piano player began to bang heavily on the keys, Dominique made her long-awaited entrance into the sanctuary. She felt like a superstar. Even though she did not make eye contact with any of the members, she knew that every eye was on her. Every step she made toward the pulpit was calculated. She walked softly, with a slight twist of her hips. Straight shoulders draped by her bulging shoulder pads, and she had a smile that was somewhere between good and evil. That was her deliberate trademark smile, the goodness to appease the saints and the evil to invoke the lustful minds and loins of the other 99 percent of the members. Dominique learned from her childhood that anyone could be lustful, regardless of age or sex, thanks to her encounter with the good colonel when she was just a developing little innocent girl that invoked indecent thoughts in his maturing mind. Men stared and gawked but could not turn away because of their masculine, innate nature, but the women looked away quickly to not seem curious or fascinated by the natural beauty that Dominique possessed.

Dominique was pleased as she stood in the pulpit and listened to the melodious voices of the choir sing one of her favorite hymns. *This is falling into place*, Dominique thought to herself. She then begin to sing along with the choir, making sure that she stepped out of the pulpit, looking toward, yet through every member of the congregation to make sure that she had the attention of all. It was commonplace for Dominique to take over leading the song, as everyone had grown accustomed to. The congregation loved to hear her sing. Her singing reminded them of when they were young and had dreams and aspirations to make it out of the hot dusty fields themselves. But that was of times past. Those tears that the old folks cried were those of sorrow for themselves that they did not or could not do better in their lives and that they were not the pretty little girl that Dominique reminded them of. Dominique touched each elderly person's hand as she passed by. Years earlier, she realized that not all tears were tears of happiness, but of sorrow, and a touch from her and the imitation smile of concern that she gave them always convinced the elderly crowd to pay even larger amounts above their normal tithe and offerings.

The men, even the ones that had been bamboozled by the self-fulfilling plans of Dominique, rose to their feet as she made her way down the aisle. Those that were duped refused to make eye contact with her, afraid that they may fall prey again in the web that they knew she was capable of weaving. The other deacons, trustees, laymen, and helpers longed to be in her grips, unaware of the consequences that came along with her attention, so they were sure to be first in line, even ahead of the women and children, to get a soft kiss on the cheek from her luscious, so-called spirit-filled lips that they so longed to have. To that naïve group of men, that kiss was code from Dominique to express an interest that she may possibly have in them. But Dominique, hardened by time and her lack of empathy for anyone, felt nothing as she laid her lips across each of their cheeks. Dominique did, however, made mental note of the weakest ones just in case she needed to trap one of them for her purposes down the road.

Dominique had been observing the actions of the younger to middle-aged women in the congregation as she sang the hymn of Zion for about six minutes. She noticed that they would sing along with her to the top of their lungs. She noticed how their backs would become a bit straighter as she passed by their aisle. She noticed how the young mother would pass her child to a nearby grandmother or aunt as she passed by and made eye contact with each and every member. Dominique noticed how some women would make sure that a wayward strand of hair was back in place or tucked in their hat as she passed by. She noticed how some women would make sure that the lose knot in their panty hose that was tied at the thigh was tightened so as not to sag as she passed by. "Here we go!" Dominique said to herself. "This congregation is a candy storefront for me, and this will be easier than I thought." Dominque sang on and on as she looked out for her next new-generation victim, a victim that had "the look." A look that was raw yet could easily be molded into a clay sculpture for her own cause. *There's one, two, three . . .*, she thought as she sang as if she was sending a soul on up to glory. As she shook their hands, Dominique gave each of her next "victims" a little scrub on the palm with her index finger, yet gently holding, not shaking their hands. Everything to Dominique had a purpose. Everything was a seed. If there was one Bible verse that she tailored to meet her own needs, it was Galatians 6:7. Dominique had planted many seeds with her next crop during that ten-minute solo. As she made her way back to her stage and finished her solo, there was not a dry eye in the congregation. Many tears had been shed from the Spirit that fell upon them, others tears of joy, and for the women in the congregation, a question of what her gentle touch of the hand could have meant. Some thought that God was going to bless them. Others had a self-fulfilling prophesy that someone of Dominique's stature and presence had paid them some form of attention. And that's exactly what Dominique was hoping for. She was hoping that their weakness and need for attention would lead them right into the palm of her hands.

Dominique knew that the congregation was ready for her sermon. They were prepped, curious, yet fascinated by the mixed messages she had sent as she paraded up and down the aisles. She had gained the attention of everyone in the church. Her solo ended, and the piano banging stopped. Dominique was ready to deliver a message to the congregation that they would never forget.

The church was filled to its capacity that day, and the spirit was high, and Dominique was at her brilliant best. She dressed herself like a Hollywood model. She charmed the audience with her beautiful melodious voice and her powerful eloquence. They were truly spellbound by her performance. After this service, Dominique felt very confident that she was on the precipice of newly awaited conquest.

"Well, Reverend Dominique, that was one of the most electrifying sermons that I have ever heard," said Bennie.

Dominique replied, "Oh, thank you, Deacon Bennie."

That afternoon, after morning worship, Deacon Bennie and his wife, Mae Bell, took Dominique to dinner as a gesture of thanks and fellowship. While chatting and exchanging laughter, Mae Bell asked to be excused to visit the ladies' room, and Dominique suggested that she would go too. When they arrived in the ladies' room, Dominique noticed Mae Bell's slip was hanging low; and with unbridled boldness, she began to assist Mae Bell by touching her hips with one hand and lifting the slip with the other. As she lifted her slip, she looked into Mae Bell's eyes and believed she saw an opening for some unchartered excitement. Mae Bell embraced Dominique, and Dominique took over the moment. She kissed Mae Bell and gently began to touch her all over. Mae Bell found herself quickly under the spell of Dominique. She moaned quietly, saying, "I have been so curious so long for this." The passion of the moment intensified as the two began to rotate their hips toward each other. Dominique, by now aggressive, touched her hips and back and gently ran her fingers through her hair. Then there was a loud thump, which interrupted the blazing passion of this visit, which also indicated someone had entered the ladies' room. They quickly recollected themselves, and with the poise of two social sophisticants, they sauntered back to the dinner table.

This was a moment that would never be forgotten. Dominique was glad that she could enlist help from the deacon. After dinner, Dominique and the deacon exchanged numbers. Dominique told him she was not leaving right then because it was getting late, and she would spend the night at a hotel.

Deacon Bennie said, "Great. I hope you rest well, and if you need us, please give us a call."

She said, "OK, will do." Just before they departed, they shook hands. Dominique's forefinger rubbed back and forth in the palm of Deacon Bennie. He smiled, and in delight, he again stated, "If you need anything, call anytime."

She said, "Last night, I was in room 312 at the motor lodge, and that's where I'll be tonight."

"OK," said Bennie.

As night falls . . .

As night fell, Dominique reflected on the events of the day. She continued to replay the bathroom event with Mae Bell over and over in her mind. So she decided she needed to figure out a way to see her before she left the next day. Her addiction to risk fed her passion to do what others would not do. As the clock struck 8:30 p.m., she picked up the phone to call Mae Bell and invited her to her room. Her strategy was to call her under the pretense of some girl talk, maybe dessert, and some social intermingling. So when she called, Deacon Bennie answered the phone. "Hello." Dominique replied and asked, "How are you, Deac?"

"Fine, and I hope you are too," said Bennie.

"I am, thank you. May I speak with Mae Bell?" said Dominique.

"Of course," he answered.

Mae Bell by now knew whom Bennie was talking to, so she rushed to answer the phone. Dominique then expressed her thanks for the afternoon, and she wanted her to know how thrilled she was over the bathroom episode. Mae Bell responded, "I too enjoyed that special moment." Dominique then asked her to come by the room for a little while since she was leaving in the morning. Mae Bell thought it was a colossal idea and said she would stop by for a minute. Dominique said, "OK, what time will you be here?" Mae Bell said, "I'll be there in forty-five minutes."

"Dominique said, "I'll be waiting."

So she started preparing herself for the arrival of Mae Bell. But the next part of her plan was to lure Deacon Bennie into a venue where she could expand the finger-rubbing-palm moment she had with him earlier that day. So she waited twenty minutes thinking by now Mae Bell would be on her way to her room. Then she called again. When the phone rang again, Bennie answered and said, "Hello."

Dominique responded, "Well, it's me again."

"I know, and Mae Bell is on her way to see you," said Bennie.

"Fine, but I really wanted to speak with you," said Dominique.

"What's up?" Bennie enthusiastically said.

Dominique responded, "Well, I asked Mae Bell to come by so I could speak to you privately for a moment."

"OK, how can I help you?" asked Bennie.

"Well, I am leaving in the morning, and I was hoping I could see you before I left," said Dominique.

He said, "That's fine. is there any particular subject you want to discuss?"

She said, "Yes, I couldn't help but acknowledge the obvious chemistry and electricity that presented themselves when we left each other, and I would love to follow through on it."

He said, "Cool. I can come by in the morning and go to work after 12:00."

She said, "That sounds nice, and I am looking forward to seeing you. I was not sure if you could do this dance."

He said, "Don't worry about whether I can dance. You just play the right song, and I'll show you I can shake, rattle, and roll."

"I like that," said Dominique.

"I'm glad you do, so I'll call in the morning, and of course this must be between us," Bennie responded.

"Of course, it'll always be. Have a good night, Deac, and I'll be waiting for you," she said.

"You too," said the deacon.

About 9:20 that evening, Mae Bell knocked on Dominique's hotel door. As Dominique opened the door, she was excited about the company of Mae Bell. Mae Bell was seductively dressed, and Dominique complimented her arresting presence. Immediately, Dominique hugged Mae Bell, and Mae Bell responded, "I have been waiting a long time for my hidden desires to be addressed." Passionately, she received the advances of Dominique as she moaned pleasurably to be kissed and touched by the leader of worship that day. Mae Bell said as she fell deeper into fleshly pleasure, "I thought you wanted dessert," and continued to sigh, expressing her consent.

Dominique said, "This is dessert, and wouldn't this be nice on the regular?"

"Yes," Mae Bell groaned.

As she continued to pleasure her lover, Dominique said, "Talk to Bennie and we could hook up like this anytime."

"Just do it, baby. You got me!" Mae Bell shouted.

"Ah, that's good to know, and I got you too," Dominique responded. The two of them exchanged pleasurable moments for the next two hours. This was particularly gratifying to Dominique because the pleasure with Mae Bell was the groundwork for a larger scheme. When Mae Bell said good night, she was completely under the spell of a new experience that continued to move her mind into pleasure that was imagined.

Dominique, the ever-calculating diva, prepared herself for the next daring experience that was scheduled the next morning. She showered, washed her hair, called housekeeping, and insisted her room be cleaned up again, expressing disdain for her room's cleanliness not meeting her standards.

Apologetically, and with dispatch, one of the room attendants recleaned her room and cleaned until she was satisfied. You see, Dominique's real purpose in all this was to make sure there was no residue or evidence whatsoever of the rather unusual episode that had been the focal point of the evening. Before retiring for the evening, she garbed herself in pajamas, bedroom slippers, and a beautiful housecoat and walked to the front desk to speak to the manager. The purpose of her visit was to personally make sure that housekeeping would not disturb her room the next morning because her meeting was too significant for interruption. It was most important to her that she controlled the environment so as to assure her next participant in carnal pleasure that the atmosphere for engagement was both conducive and copacetic.

The next morning, Dominique rose bright and early, anticipating the arrival of the eager deacon. Her hair was soft and silky, and she had rose petals on the floor and on the bed. While music played softly, there was a knock at the door. It was Deacon Bennie. Having made all matters clear before his arrival, she did not hesitate to reach for him and he for her. In the throes of romantic ecstasy, the two of them engaged themselves with each other for the next two hours. It was such a special moment for Bennie that when he left, nothing Dominique could have requested, he would not seek to fulfill. Needless to say, Bennie was looking down the road for repeated engagements, but Dominique's interest had expired the moment it ended. Deacon Bennie left the motel room expressing his love and his recommendation for her to become the next pastor. Within one week, Dominique became the pastor of the star community church.

Days after becoming the pastor, Dominique became rather fatigued of Bennie's unwelcomed advances but understood that she needed him for her work. Bennie planned to be more comfortable with Dominique, while she had become more uncomfortable with him. Bennie quickly saw that money was very important to Dominique and sought to use this as a method to get closer to her.

One day, Bennie knocked on Dominique's door. "Bennie, what is it that you want? I am extremely busy. You know I send for you when I need you."

Bennie was red with anger inside. He hated how Dominique spoke to him, but he managed to muster a smile to mask the emasculation he was always the brunt of around Dominique.

"I have a business proposition for you. You have been so good to me over the years. I have been lying awake in bed, thinking about the perfect time to share this business opportunity with you."

Dominique didn't flinch. Even though she was salivating at the thought of another opportunity and another stack of green to her growing wealth, she knew that she could never let anyone see her hunger for more.

"What is it, Bennie? I really have a pressing matter to which I must attend."

Dominique was bursting at the seams with anticipation like stars in a faraway galaxy glistening in a moonlit sky. She blocked out every invasive thought in her mind at the mere mention of gain. Bennie felt as confident as he had ever felt in his life. Finally, he had gained advantage over someone in his despondent life, only if for a moment. Someone, especially someone like Dominique, was finally interested in what he had to say. This moment seemed unreal to him. Only if he could just relish in it for the rest of his life would he be a fulfilled man. An ounce of respect felt good, and Bennie thought that he could get used to this.

"I am so glad you asked," Bennie responded with a sense of arrogance and long-awaited entitlement.

"I didn't ask!" Dominique retorted in a way that illustrated how insulted she was with the mere thought of Bennie even thinking that she needed something from him.

Dominique had such a hold over Bennie that he actually was convinced that Dominique's question earlier was really not even a question.

"I . . . uhh . . . have a meeting in the morning with a businessman who is from across the water that I met when I lived up the road a few years back."

Dominique listened intently.

"He has a business that has been largely successful, and I have a chance to get a piece of the pie since he has known and trusted me over the years. And with your brains, I figured that you could carefully analyze and translate, if you will, this great plan of his. Who knows? You may even become interested yourself."

Why is he really telling me? Dominique thought to herself. "I will go along with you, but only because I have another stop to make afterward. Just tell me where you will be, and I will meet you there."

"That will be fine, just fine! I am so glad that . . ."

"Bennie, could you close the door on your way out? I have a lot to do for the church today."

Bennie pivoted without saying a word, almost like a child that had been admonished for bad behavior. Even so, he smiled from within. Even though Dominique treated him badly, he was still drawn to her. She always managed to hypnotize him into some kind of trance where it didn't really matter what she used him for, just as long as he could see her to satisfy his need for attention. It didn't matter to him that it was negative attention. He was just grateful that she took the time to see him for the three and a half minutes that she allowed him to spend with her. Perhaps this business venture would win her over, and he would see how valuable he was after all.

As Dominique was preparing for her day as she did just like clockwork, she heard a knock at the door.

"Hello, Pastor, I am so glad that you could meet with me today. After your sermon on last Sunday, I just knew that I had to come see you. I have been lost for so long, not knowing which way to go. I just had to speak with you. After your message, I knew that you would understand the burdens of my life."

"This is truly my pleasure." Dominique was radiating with happiness. She recognized her member Rita right away. She felt as if she had hit the jackpot. She had longed to connect with some of the younger women in the church that would help her build her brand and expand her base. Thoughts of her mother using her gender to navigate through life popped up again in Dominique's head. Dominique love to counsel members. This was her opportunity to help parishioners while simultaneously brainwashing the ones that could serve a purpose in her army. Dominique had never been moved by the appearance of anyone. But Dominique saw Rita as one that could become a part of her team. She remembered this young woman well. This one was the first hand she grabbed while she was singing her electrifying solo and marching up and down the aisles. This was the one that had the look in her eye, a look of uncertainty and a look of malleability that would conform to Dominique's whims, wishes, and wants. As attractive as this woman was, Dominique knew she could surely use her on her team and possibly for a whole lot more.

"I love to come to church, Pastor, and I love to hear you speak the Word. I was especially glad to hear you say that God loves us all, and He expects us to love Him and others regardless of who they are."

"Love can be a beautiful thing." Dominique continued to admire the young woman's vibrancy. Dominique was smitten by her boldness to speak on such a taboo subject: love. "Beauty is a creation of God. Love is a creation of God. Our minds do not determine who we love. Our hearts do." By looking at her member, Dominique knew why some men cannot resist some women.

"Pastor, I should probably leave now. I really apologize for talking about love. You see, in our household, it was such a taboo subject. It was a word that symbolized weakness, so it wasn't used much in our family. I am falling in love with someone, but I do not know which way to turn!"

Rita rose to leave and began walking hurriedly to the door.

One thing Dominique mastered was how to be observant and how to be quick. Dominique stood up with her, gently grabbed her hand, and walked with her to the door. Through her years of counseling, Dominique knew not to be too forceful or overbearing while speaking with members. They stopped just adjacent to her closet, which contained the finest silks and other imports from abroad. Dominique thought that she had hit the jackpot. Finally, one of the members she had "recruited" was right there in her office, ready to be shaped like a lifeless mound of clay. Dominique felt that she could love everybody or no one depending on the situation. Dominique waited patiently to see what the member's next move would be. But in an instant, the member burst out in a sea of tears.

"It's OK," Dominique said as she gently hugged the member to let her express her overwhelming moment of relief. You cry for as long as you want. This embrace continued for several minutes. Dominique treaded lightly with this delicate girl, so she began to rub her back and comfort her even more. The member enjoyed the feel of someone so strong and passionate in their beliefs. The member slowly responded by placing her hand gingerly on Dominique's back to symbolize her comfort in Dominique's arms.

Dominique seized the opportunity and quoted one of the hundreds of scriptures that she memorized, "Let him kiss me with the kisses of his mouth: for thy love is better than wine."

Rita looked intently into Dominique's eyes. Their lips met with the gentleness of a baby's breath and the naturalness of Adam and Eve naked in the Garden of Eden before the serpent slithers onto the scene. The dancing of their tongues supplemented by the scripture of Solomon reassured for the member that a kiss is natural, especially since it was in the Bible. Their passionate embrace led them into the closet beside which they were standing for what seemed like eternity. They gently lowered their bodies onto the chaise lounge that was as soft and supple as the lovely creatures that inhabited it. They explored each other in such a way that fulfilled the fantasy that they both shared. Soon their bodies were wet with the moisture of the passion that seemed to have dripped from their hearts. The intensity of the moment concluded like a volcano filled with hot molten lava erupting onto a grassy countryside below.

Soon Dominique and Rita found themselves again and rose from the pillar of pleasure in the closet that housed their bodies. The member left, and there was not a word spoken between Dominique and the member who had quickly fallen in Dominique's tangled web that had often been mistaken for love. The member walked out of Dominique's office like a sinner freshly baptized in the pool of the Holy Ghost fire. She was beaming and excited about the prospect of becoming a part of Dominique's inner circle. She had gotten what she was looking for: her answer to her burning question about love. She could not wait to see Dominique again, for she knew that Dominique was feeling the same way as she. But the member couldn't had been more mistaken, for the moment the member floated out of the door on a flurry of clouds, Dominique had begun eating the plate of chicken wings that Bennie had secretly left on her desk for her, wondering about the businessman she was supposed to meet tomorrow.

As night falls . . .

Dominique had been restless all night. The thought of money made her salivate at the prospects of becoming richer and bigger than life itself. She wondered what this business venture could be. The stock market? Livestock? Liquor? A counterfeiting operation? Dominique couldn't wait to find out, and for the first time in her life, she was actually excited about seeing Bennie in the morning. Whatever this opportunity was, Dominique was going to be a part of it. She even thought that she would eliminate Bennie if need be. Perhaps she should take the member from earlier today with her or maybe wait until the next one filed into her office with a similar story about that love business; she would decide later that morning.

"Maybe it would be a good idea to take that member with me," Dominique said aloud in a room filled only with her thoughts and the darkness of the night. "Bennie would be twice as gullible and three times more usable with him getting the shaft from me and this girl." Dominique marveled at her brilliance. "I've already captured her body, and that means her mind is not too far behind." Dominique never seemed to amaze herself when it came to the power of using people for her own personal gains and without an ounce of regret or sympathy for her victims.

Dominique was sure that she was the first to arrive. She always remembered the old adage "The early bird gets the worm." Dominique wanted to ensure that she observed the mannerisms of this potential business client as he entered the room. Details were important. His style, swag, and even how he scanned the room could all be important details to his astuteness. From Bennie's description, her head was spinning with images of what he looked like. She knew he was tall, about six foot two, was medium build, and would have on attire appropriate for the occasion. His trademark glasses would also help her to identify this mysterious gentleman whom she envisioned would catapult her to her respective place in society. Dominique walked to the meeting place, scanned the room, and noticed that neither Bennie nor he was there.

Good, she thought. She knew that she had arrived just in time to observe the gentleman walk in. Dominique walked in and took her seat. She took one last scan of the room. She didn't notice that Bennie and the businessman had already arrived before her and were sitting in an obscure corner in the dimly lit meeting place.

Dominique had not been aware of her surroundings and the fact that this meeting could make or break her rise to the top. She subtly caught Bennie's eye. She dared not move. As a woman, that would have been totally improper, and it would have revealed just how surprised she was to have been so wrong about the timing of her arrival. Bennie and the businessman stood up to make their way over to Dominique's table. Bennie had a near-smirk on his face, with the reason being twofold. First, he had a chance to see the beautiful Dominique again; and second, he finally felt that for the first time in his life, he was successful in his dealings with Dominique by beating her to the spot. Dominique was livid, however. How could her timing be so off? Surely, the businessman would see her as someone not worthy of a business deal, but she quickly brushed that idea off and snapped back to her reality very quickly.

"Dominique," Bennie said in a sophisticated manner as he continued to approach her table.

"Hello, Bennie, it is so good to see you again," she replied, knowing in her heart that she didn't care if she saw him or not, but Dominique was good at hiding her true feelings.

"Dominique, this is Mr. Sampson, the fine gentleman we spoke of the other day."

Mr. Sampson reached out his hand, and Dominique responded by offering her hand in the fashion of the day for a greeting.

"Hello. Pleased to meet you, Mr. Sampson. I have heard so much about you."

Bennie chimed in, "Shall we get down to business?"

They all sat slowly, certain as to not exhibit any haste to continue.

Bennie, still with his head in the clouds, was extremely excited about how the meeting was going so far. "I am so glad that we could meet. I have been wondering how . . ."

"Mr. Sampson, I am a businesswoman," Dominique interrupted. "And I can tell that you are a businessman. I know that we are in two different fields, for I am a minister, and you are a worldly man. However, I do not see where this should impact our business relationship in any way. I am a minister, but I also know that business comes first. So let's not beat around the bush. What is your business proposition?"

"Dominique," Mr. Sampson started, "I like the way you think. Not too hasty and not too slow. You like it cut right down the middle to the heart of the matter."

"Oh yes, I do," she replied.

"Dominique, I am a man of means. I have been on the circuit for quite some time. All of my businesses, whether on the black-hand side or white-hand side, work, if you know what I mean."

Dominique did not respond or nod. That was just another strategy to control victims with words, and she was not going to fall for it.

Mr. Sampson continued, "Dominique, I need you for my business. I am quite successful, but I am missing a little something. I am looking for a front man, if you will. I remain looking for a partner that is cold enough to be cutthroat, but hot enough to burn them alive. My business success depends upon a client's willingness to use my product. This product will make you rich and will make me richer."

Dominique's eyes danced with excitement, for she already knew what this "product" was. And that's exactly what she wanted to hear. Dominique's mind lived on the edge. Her thoughts teetered from mischief to ministry. Either one could equally satisfy her. The thrill alone of living two different lives left her full of energy that she would be willing to burn off whatever means that made her happy.

Mr. Sampson, who already knew that Dominique would be in, went on, "We could run the entire South. We could run this whole country with what I have. Confederate or Yankee, colored or white, rich or poor. It won't matter. My plan is to take a couple of dollars that I came into from the cocaine that I used to sell to that bottling company up the road and take those funds to open up ministries all over this country. And believe me. People will be running to go to *your* churches. Yes, your churches, Dominique. At night.

"Worshipping at the church and leaving an offering will allow members to receive a 50 percent discount on the first two drinks and 25 percent the rest of the night. We would inflate the cost, and most are not able to count anyway. Besides, they can't get our services anywhere around here.

"People are tired from working all day to have to get up and go to church on Sundays and then to have to sit there all day. Instead, you can open up what I will call this church of convenience. People can come to worship anytime they want to. Then they can go over to the other business and get a drink and get as wet as they want, if they like. Business people will be glad to attend your church as well. Pretty soon, your congregations will be so large that you won't even know what to do with them. And no one will know you will be behind all of the Holy Water you will be selling to the people who just want to, shall we say, relax.

"I am telling you, Dominque. If you want your ministry to grow, you have to be a radical. You have to get into this with me. Just think about all of those hard-working women who tend to children all day and need to serve the Lord more than just on a Sunday, you see. They need to be able to drop in whenever the spirit hits them so that they can be rejuvenated. Or if they choose, they can attend church at night. And this Holy Water will be just what these women need to make them feel like women. It will make them want go on home to their old dusty, dirty, musky men to make them feel like men again. And just think. If you play your cards right, think of all the women you will draw close to you. You could probably get them to do just about anything with one sip of this. Imagine how tasty their lips would be and how gentle their breath would be with just a taste of what you would be serving them.

This is what you have been waiting for, Dominique. This juice will set you apart from all others, male or female. You will have a full-time ministry, a full-time business, and if you work these women like I saw you do the other Sunday during that electrifying sermon, you can open up a little side business utilizing their other services and talents, if you know what I mean.

"You go ahead and think about where you want to open these churches. I have the capital. I just need a captain who will steer this ship all the way down the sea of success. This business will also allow you the flexibility to move and go how you want to, with no questions asked by any law. They would probably even escort a pretty gal minister like you in the dark of night. You could transport your own product as you see fit, and for all anyone knows, you are simply going to your congregations to hold your services."

Dominique could not believe what she was hearing. Being a nationally known minister is what she dreamed of. But even she was stunned at the magnitude this ministry could grow and the many branches that could be grown from one ministry: money, alcohol, power, and even souls saved along the way do not sound like a bad plan, especially for her. She figured that she could, on average, probably start one ministry per month. And by the end of the year, she could have twelve. And with all of that money coming in, she could be the richest woman in the world. She wanted to get up and scream but dared not to. She would wait and do a holy dance when she got home and would celebrate over a glass a gin.

"I'm not so sure this will work," she said coldly. "Besides, I am not even sure that I want a business partner."

"My dear, you want a business partner. You will take whatever partner you can get in order to get what you want. Isn't that so?" Mr. Sampson said, looking over invisible glasses that a person would think were on his face.

"Mr. Sampson, I would need a day or so to think about this. Going into the business with you, a stranger, is extremely risky. I need to be willing to take that risk, for I do not want to be financially ruined nor publicly humiliated by some two-bit hustler whom I never heard of."

As she drove home to think about an offer she couldn't refuse, all she could think about was how she would be a worldwide star and how she would be a pioneer in not just the field of ministry, but the women's ministry. She had to find a pulpit where she can think and absorb all the positive energy that was flowing. She pulled up to an old church where she could have easy access and not be noticed, except by the dark that covered the night's secrets. The dollar signs began to dance lively in her head as she thought about what she could do with her newfound fame and fortune. She wanted to conquer the world. She wanted everyone to know who she was. On the outside, she was a picture of perfection. Her spiritual life was in a mess, and many came to hear what she had to say. She had a message. She had a message and a solution for every situation imaginable. Reeling them in would be easy. Now that she had the chance to go nationwide with her message and her mission, she could hardly contain herself. She was on the cusp of exploding with the anticipation of being not only the next big thing but the only big thing with what she had in mind of doing. She knew that saving souls would be easy. She just had to be careful not to misstep and make a fatal mistake.

She knew that a mistake or a lapse in judgment could prove to be fatal to her existence and precarious to her ambitions. All this energy that she felt at the thought of herself began to plague her body, and it felt as if bolts of energy were flowing in all the nerves, capillaries, and arteries of her body instead of the warm blood that fueled her ingenuous mind. This allowed her to visualize what her life would be. All this tension caused her to blossom with pellets of moisture that covered her soft, delicate skin. Whenever Dominique had moments such as these, all she could think of was relieving these tensions as sensually as possible. She thought about the experience she had in her closet with the new troubled member that she counseled just a few hours ago as she kneeled humbly in the pulpit to pray. Instead of praying, her juxtaposed thoughts took her elsewhere. She began to feel the glistening moisture that bubbled on her skin, and she began rubbing every part of her body as she laid her body completely down at the altar. It was almost as if she was in a meditative state, for she heard not even the cantankerous, cacophonous melody of the crickets that were just below the window that would have jarred anyone out of a state of self. The tension of excitement that had built up within her needed to be released in order for her to feel the calm that she was used to. As she lay there, her hand began to stroke her smooth skin more intimately as she began to feel the tension subside. Dominique began to moan as she began to think about the wonderful events in her life that were on the cusp of blooming and the warm feeling of her hands gliding over her skin to relax her fully. Those few minutes that Dominique enjoyed her own company seemed like an eternity once Dominique came back to herself. The sweat that once entrenched her body had now retreated back into the pores from which they had sprung, and an internal sigh of relief was the signal that she could regain focus on the mission that lie ahead.

Dominique was a true businesswoman. She relished the fact that she could promote her ministry and open up establishments that would support her growing churches while satisfying her business sense with these liquor houses. Dominique knew of no other women who were in a questionable business yet still successful. Dominique also knew that the new girl that came to her memory in the pulpit could be a front girl to run the business. Besides, Dominique knew that she already had captivated that girl's mind and body.

Pulling the puppet strings would be easy. She knew that this girl would be willing to do anything she had in mind. Dominique had to get into action quickly and had to formulate who would be on this mission with her. She trusted no one and only need a few loyal soldiers to get down in the trenches for her. Dominique quickly composed herself, for she had to prepare for another meeting with Mr. Sampson on Friday. In the meantime, however, Dominique knew she had to work on who would be loyal to her and how to eliminate the same as soon as their use for her had expired.

Dominique knew of no one who had their own business. The thought of being taken seriously had Dominique walking on cloud nine. This upcoming meeting that Dominique had set up with Mr. Sampson had a dual purpose. First, Dominique was eager to begin her new role as a CEO. Second, and more importantly, it was important for Mr. Sampson to know that she could be trusted. Dominique was confident that the more she met with Mr. Sampson, the more he would be captivated by her, which meant that she could run circles around him. Dominique knew, however, that she must learn all she could about Mr. Sampson because a businessman like him was surely always thinking. And if he was thinking, he had to certainly be thinking about her. What Dominique hadn't figured out was if these thoughts she was having about Mr. Sampson was taking up as much time as the thoughts he was having about her.

At the next meeting, Dominique wanted to arrive earlier than she did the last time. Even though Dominique enjoyed the topic of discussion, she also wanted to reestablish herself with him, for she felt that the blunder of being the last to arrive at the last meeting revealed a sense of misinterpretation on her part. She would not let this happen again. Through this redemption, she would reinvent herself as the shot caller.

Oh good, Dominique thought to herself as she arrived at the restaurant. She was thrilled to see that Mr. Sampson had not arrived yet, so she had a few more moments to prepare herself mentally for the pivotal experience that was about to take place. Dominique had already begun to formulate in her mind what she thought this business would look like. She wanted to attract people from all walks of life and from every community. Race didn't matter. Money did. That was how she was going to grow her ministry and run these businesses simultaneously without the two ever meeting. Dominique knew that this would not pose a problem because she had several internal affairs that were alive within her that she managed to keep separate. Dominique was very excited. She barely even noticed Mr. Sampson walking up to her table. But because she learned long ago to always be aware of her surroundings, Dominique developed a keen sense of awareness of what was ever present around her.

"Lester," Dominique said as she took it upon herself to call Mr. Sampson by his first name, an important step in her gaining control over such an interesting study such as Mr. Sampson. She had seen his type before. It would be next to impossible for her to break him, but she knew she had to. She hadn't completely figured out how, but she knew one day that she would be a "Mr. Sampson." Perhaps even Mr. Sampson himself.

"Dominique," Mr. Sampson retorted as he looked closely at her incomparable beauty, all while trying to look through her exterior that protected all her hidden secrets. He had seen them all before, or so he thought. But he knew he had to tread carefully because this one was different. "How nice it is to be graced with your lovely presence again."

"I am clearly delighted that you have agreed to meet with me," Dominique said slowly as she looked over her own eyes to give Mr. Sampson a false glance into her persona.

"It is definitely my pleasure," he said as he reached for her wrist to kiss it with his soft, delicate lips that have melted the hearts and minds of plenty lady victims. As his lips gently visited her wrist for that moment, he wondered how many other men have auditioned for her attention throughout the years.

Dominique and Mr. Sampson had at least one similarity in common. They were consistently suspicious of anyone, especially beautiful people with means.

"I am caught off guard that you would want to meet so soon, yet I was just waiting for the right moments for us to, uh, get started." Mr. Sampson was long ready to get started, but a part of his own tactic was to stall long enough for a potential businesses partner to contact him. This would give him a glimpse into their psyche and urgency to gain what he has.

"Lester," Dominique said as she sipped on a little bourbon with a twist of lemon, a lady's drink, whether they are on the clock or not, "I am going to get right to it. I will be your business partner or your business lady, but on a few conditions."

"I see," said Mr. Sampson.

Dominique continued, "I can see where this business will benefit both of us." Dominique refrained from mentioning opening other churches, for this would reveal a false sense of desperation from her that did not exist within her.

"It will," he said. Mr. Sampson was a man of few words. He enjoyed hearing others speak. This allowed him to further dissect the woman sitting directly across him.

"I have opened businesses many times before. Now once the business opens, there will be a variety of entertainment that patrons can enjoy. An evening drink with the company of others, a little companionship, and other social activities. I am going to call it the Black Jack Den," Dominique said.

"Dominique, the Black Jack Den will be your baby. It will be yours to run as you choose. And if you would like, and if there is someone whom you trust enough, you can even have a front person to run it for you, or you can run it yourself. I don't think that you would want to run it yourself, would you? Besides, your congregation can't see you two ways, and you benefit financially from it."

"Absolutely not. I have already trained a girl who would be perfect for it."

"Wonderful. Now how this will work, Dominique, is that you and I will split proceeds 50 percent from the women, wine, and whatever grows from this business. I know that the Black Jack Den will only be the beginning of what we can do together. We can rule this business world and set ourselves up for the rest of our lives. A dollar for you and a dollar for me. And you will be running this business in absentia. I trust you 100 percent. Bennie has never steered me wrong before, and you have shown me nothing but a business professional."

"Lester, I am so excited about this. I know that I can make this business grow, and I know that plenty of money will come in, especially once I stock it with the finest products from which to select."

"I know you can, Dominique. Now for the Black Jack Den, you have the front girl ready. I will provide the liquor that the patrons will buy by the glass and the comforts that any man or woman for that matter can enjoy. Any subsequent business that we open, I will provide the location and the alcohol, and you provide the women. Fifty-fifty right down your middle, Dominique."

"It's a deal, sir."

"Deal."

"We'll be in touch the day after tomorrow after I secure the key." And with that, Mr. Sampson stood up, pivoted, and left the restaurant quickly. In a flash, he was gone.

Dominique was left sitting there, stunned. She was stunned that she was about to begin stacking her dollars and more stunned at the fact that she was left sitting in a restaurant without even having the opportunity to have the last word.

Meanwhile, Rita had longed for an excuse to see Dominique again. When she got the message from one of the old trustees that it was urgent that she meet with Dominique on Tuesday, Rita's heart almost burst with anticipation. She had never felt like this before. It was a strange feeling, a feeling of uncertainty as to where this strange feeling may carry her. Rita considered herself a good Christian girl, one who tried to live by the good book. She wondered if she could be falling in love with Dominique, and she quickly tried to dismiss this notion. Yet the notion was too stubborn. It would not uproot from where it had taken hold of her mind and her heart. Rita decided that she was going to follow her heart and prayed that Dominique was captivated by presence her too.

As Rita walked down the dusty road, several cars slowed down to stop and offer her a ride. Even though she was inclined to do so, Rita wanted to be lost in her thoughts at the anticipation of seeing Dominique again. Rita had no idea what the meeting was about. Perhaps she should make up some reason, some problem, or some issue that need immediate attention. Perhaps she should look worn from the walk. Or maybe she should make a dramatic entrance to Dominique's office by sobbing hysterically about being scorned by a beau or ostracized by her family for some reason. Rita decided against it. Instead, Rita found a burst of confidence and decided that she was going to walk into Dominique's study quietly and be patient about what this meeting could possibly be about. Rita picked up her pace as she saw a storm cloud headed in her direction. She quickly saw an old outhouse that was unoccupied. She quickly stepped in to freshen up a bit. In another two hundred yards, Rita would have answers to many of her questions.

"Sister Rita! I am so glad that you could make it. I was a little concerned if the weather was going to hold out, but I am so glad that you pressed your way on out to the church today," Dominique said with as much sincerity as she could muster.

"Hello," was the only response that a starry-eyed Rita could whisper, even after all the different scenarios that she imagined as she entered Dominique's office.

Dominique could sense fear, just like a cat that preys upon a mouse that already knows he has lost the battle.

"Rita, it has been so long, I have been thinking about you, and I hope that you and your family are well. I am so glad that you and your family are dedicated to the cause of the church." Dominique learned the art of conversation from watching her mother long ago. Dominique was a master at making obtuse statements that would lead another conversationalist to reveal what was really on their mind. To Dominique, people were like chess pieces. Her opponent's move would definitely lead to their inevitable capture or at least the opponent's resignation from the game when he or she sees they can't win.

"Oh yes, it is my pleasure," which was the only standard response a nervous Rita could think of, seeing that she was clouded by Dominique's beauty. "I was actually hoping to meet weekly with you anyway. There are several things that are going on in my life. I don't know how to begin to even manage it. It's quite overwhelming."

Dominique's mind immediately switched from chess to fishing. *It can't be this easy*, Dominique thought to herself and hoped she didn't say out loud. *I just landed this fish on the hook without even having my pole in the water that long,* she continued to think. Dominique also knew that Rita was mesmerized by her and was praying for another exploratory session of the mind, body, and spirit. But Dominique knew that Jesus had a Gone Fishin' sign hanging on his door, and Rita's prayer wouldn't be heard today.

"Yes, life can be quite a challenge, my child, but it is truly about how you manage it. In order to find yourself, you have to lose yourself." Dominique impressed herself sometimes with little quips she could come up with at any given moment without any notice or forethought.

Rita replied, "I do! I do feel so lost."

"Not in that sense of the word, Rita."

"Well, what do you mean?"

"Sometimes, especially when we are young, we never know what direction life will take us. Therefore, we have to explore different options. But your prayer has to be that these options do not take you off course with the Lord. Have you ever lived on your own, or have you ever worked before, Rita?"

"I have helped out on the farm, and I have worked in Ms. Lucy Bell's home greeting guests, but that's about all I've done outside of the church," she replied.

This was music to Dominique's ears. All she could think about was running the business and building her church brand. A virgin to the world that is hidden by the cover of night was all that she needed. Dominique carefully prepared her words.

"Rita, you need to get out and explore the world and explore life. It's not a sin to live. It's not a sin to sample the offerings of life as you discover who you are. You are such a fine young woman." Dominique was hoping that Rita would misunderstand the double entendre and think that she was referring to her physical appearance. Even though Rita was an attractive woman, Dominique was not thinking about her physical appearance but of her youthful qualities. Dominique did, however, want to ease Rita's mind into the night session that was held in her office with her the other night without even speaking of it. Dominique loved misinterpretations, but only if they would help her cause.

Rita could hardly wait to respond. "I have been longing to do just that. What should I do first? I could pack up and leave home!"

Dominique was almost dumbfounded by such a juvenile response. "No, sister, that is too drastic of a first step." Dominique chuckled as she tried to lighten the mood and give her a sense of relief of the foolishness she just heard.

"Rita, what I am attempting to do in my ministry is reach those who are lost. I believe you would be great in helping me with my cause to bring souls to salvation."

"That sounds like something I could do!" Rita replied. She knew that saving souls would get her even closer to Dominique, as she sat, still waiting for Dominique to bring up the impromptu rendezvous that they experienced in the closet the other day. Rita would do anything for Dominique, and Dominique knew it. "What do I need to do first?"

Dominique hated eagerness, for eagerness leads to mistakes. But Dominique was willing to overlook Rita's young mind because she needed her.

"Rita, you have to be committed to anything you start. Quitting is not an option. You have to see things through, no matter the outcome. You have to believe that and prove it."

"That is the best lesson that I have ever learned. I have given up on several things before. That's probably why I cannot find myself. Please just tell me how I can start helping you save souls, and I will do it."

As night falls . . .

Maybe this is chess, Dominique thought. Dominique loved the nighttime when everything is quiet and peaceful. She had envisioned this entire conversation with Rita last night, probably while Rita was still asleep, or better yet, while Rita was dreaming about her. Dominique was so confident in herself, she felt that she could dream up any scenario, and it would happen. The nighttime brings about stillness in the atmosphere. This stillness allows objects to be captured because they are motionless for just long enough to get your hand around them or even your mind around a troubling problem. Dominique was so glad she overheard many of the white men talk about history and math growing up. They all tied it back to money and making lots of it. She remembered an old white man, who was extremely wealthy, come into the home where her mother was working and where she was running around as a very young child. The rich old man was asked, "How did you acquire so much wealth?"

"Well," the old man said slowly, "I just think about what that Frenchman said hundreds of years ago while he was figuring it all out himself: 'I think, therefore I am.' I see myself as money, so therefore, I am money. I live money. I make money."

Dominique appreciated her upbringing. Her upbringing helped her to stay focused. And right now, her focus was money.

Dominique continued, "This assignment, Rita, will be one that is extremely important. It will be all about you. What you do will control the success of the uh, souls, that we can reach."

Rita nodded as she listened attentively.

Dominique added, "I have a little business venture that I have started. This business venture will certainly help the church grow. It will be a place for church members and nonchurchgoers to go and relax. Think about it for a minute, Rita, how peaceful the night is. It's still. It's quiet. That is the time when we need to let lose the troubles of the day, to go and relax, and to let our hair down." Dominique took her hair out of her tight bun, swung it, and let it flow across her shoulders for effect. Rita's eyes gazed at her dark wavy locks, which sent Rita into a semiconscious, hypnotic state. Dominique's voice jarred her back to the present.

Dominique leaned in and said quietly, "And you can be a part of it. In this little spot, there will be music playing quietly, a little jazz gospel originated from jazz, you know, and a little spirit to fill the place. The spirit comes in many forms and fashions. The spirit I'm speaking of is liquefied, and you can pour it right into a glass, sip, listen to jazz, and relax. Even Jesus knew how to relax, for he turned water into wine. Thank you, Jesus! Jesus! Jesus!" Dominique exclaimed for effect, waved her hand, and then gently touched Rita's knee.

"Rita, this is an opportunity of a lifetime for you. This opportunity will open a million doors for you." Dominique stared at Rita intently with her dark, deep, dreamy eyes. "You will be in charge of who comes in and who comes out. It will almost be like your business. You will be who they see, and you will be who they want to see when they come back. Think about how much our men work on a daily basis. Here, they will be able to come and release the toils of the day. They will be able to have a spirit and to be stimulated mentally and physically, Rita. Perhaps you are not mature enough for all it takes to win the hearts and minds of sinners, and it is important that you are in order to help build our business. Why don't you go home and think about it, or better yet, I think that I better do it myself. I have seen cracks in your maturity already . . ."

"Pastor, I will do anything in the name of building the church, and I see how I can find myself all at the same time. I know that I am your girl. People tell me I'm beautiful all the time. I will even fill in in any way possible if need be. Plus, I have several cousins and sisters who would be willing to help."

"Rita, I think I've changed my mind, and I haven't seen your cousins or sisters. Image is everything. It could make or break me."

"Everyone says they are just as beautiful, I tell you, and they too are looking to find themselves and to make their mark in the world."

"I think you have convinced me, dear Rita, however, I will need to meet your sisters. I normally don't meet strangers, but under the circumstances, and if they are anything like you, they may be just what I need, I mean, we need to get started."

"I won't let you down, Pastor."

"Good, meet me here on Friday morning. I am so eager to help you, Rita, and you are well on your way." Dominique reached in to give Rita a gentle, light kiss on the lips to signify her appreciation for her commitment to this endeavor. Anything more would send Rita into some abyss void of thought and rationale. So a peck would be all she needed right now. Plus, Rita would be trying to work her way up for more of Dominique's affection, which would place Rita right in the palm of Dominique's hand.

Rita left Dominique's office gleaming at the fact that the pastor sill showed her love and affection. Rita knew that she was not misreading all Dominique's cues. She knew they were for real. Rita could not wait to be the pastor's girl, and she even gained an air of confidence on her way home. Everyone who saw Rita walking knew that there was something different about her walk. It seemed to be a bit lighter than it was just a few hours ago. Rita could feel her life taking a turn from nothing to something. Someone who was as important as Dominique chose her to help her with her ministry by way of this new business venture. She knew that Dominique trusted her, so because of this, she would tell no one. She would only speak with those that Dominique approved for her to speak with on this venture. Rita knew that she had to be careful not to lose her spot. Rita just imagined all the girls who would love to be important or as lucky as she was. Rita thought that running a business for Dominique would be every girl's dream. She would get to meet important people. She would get to be up front like the pastor. She would get to greet important people, and to top it off, she would get to represent Dominique. Who knows, Rita thought. She was beginning to think that she and Dominique could be partners in not only this business but also others. She could envision her and Dominique arm in arm meeting important people while building up church memberships at the same time. Rita was so caught up in her own world, she didn't even notice that the rainstorm had soaked her clothes and hair and had pasted it to her body like freshly made papier-mache.

"That was easier than I thought. Tomorrow, I will contact Mr. Sampson and let him know that we are ready for our first establishment." Dominique gathered her things and headed for home. By this time, the rain had subsided, and she began to imagine the rapid pace in which these businesses could grow. She also thought about Rita and how, by the time she was Rita's age, she could philander anybody, especially a man, into doing anything she wanted. She almost felt sorry for Rita. Almost. She felt sorry that no one had taught her the game of life when she was a little girl. Dominique felt sorry for her, but not sorry enough that Rita's unfortunate life would derail her own plans.

"Rita! What has happened to you?" her older yet just as beautiful sister, Hattie, exclaimed as she walked in the door. "You are soaking wet! Ain't nobody that important to be meeting in no rain!"

"If you knew what I was doing, you wouldn't be talking to the only girl in the family that is an entrepreneur like that," replied Rita calmly.

"You must be crazy. That rain has gotten to your head. You were just at the altar falling all out. You are not an entrepreneur or however you say it. Girl, go on and get away from here."

"OK, I will. I take that it was a mistake to mention your name." Rita spun on her heals and pretended that she was really going to walk out of the door.

"Hold on. What did you say?"

"I said that I had mentioned your name. But if you are not interested . . ."

"Girl, just tell me!"

"Well, I was just meeting with Pastor Dominique. And she really likes me and thinks that I can be good for the ministry. So she asked if I could help her out running a little store that she has. In the evenings."

"An evening store? You know stores are closed by 5:00. And besides, who shops after 5:00 anyway?"

"It's not going to be a store for shopping. It's going to be more of a place for resting, relaxation, and unwinding after work. The pastor is so busy, and she so desperately needed my help. She asked me to help her out, and how much of an opportunity it would be for me. You know I am trying to get out of this place anyway. And so are you. This is our opportunity. Besides, we look way too good to be wasting away year after year and not taking full advantage of it. You can stay around here if you want too. I have big dreams. I am going to make it out of here. I will just tell the pastor that you are not interested, and you want to continue to iron sheets all day. Fine with me."

"Don't you dare!" Hattie yelled as she lunged toward Rita in an aggressive yet playful way. "You ain't leaving me here to rot away. Tell her I'll do it."

"I already did."

"How did you know?"

"Because I sleep with your snoring tail every night. That's how!"

The sisters both proceeded to laugh because Rita was right. She knew her sister up and down. They had spent too many countless hours not to know each other. They were really all the other had. One didn't make a step without the other following behind. Right or wrong, good or bad. They always stuck together. Perhaps had they not been so close, Hattie would have inquired more about what the job entailed. But she trusted her sister so much, she didn't even bother. Rita had her convinced. Just like that, in a matter of hours, Dominique had recruited two unsuspected virgin minds to delve into the dark side. They were like little mice, not even aware that there was a cat stalking behind the bushes waiting to pounce on them for Sunday evening's supper.

As night falls . . .

Rita and Hattie rested well that night, especially Rita. She knew what the job entailed, and she couldn't wait to get started. She had never felt so empowered before, nor had she been asked to run a business in her life. Saturday night could not get there quick enough. Rita was so excited, and she couldn't wait to get all dressed up and meet new people. Rita fell asleep through the snoring of her sister, and the last image that she saw dancing in her head was Dominique.

"Hattie! Are you ready? We are going to be late. We are supposed to be meeting the pastor at the church at 7:00 to go over our new jobs tonight so that we can be at the Fox Trot by 9:00. I am not going to be late on account of you being slow. Let's go!" Rita and Hattie caught a ride with Old Man Frank who was going that way. They were so thrilled that they didn't have to walk in the dust. They would have rode with the devil had he driven by. They were so excited on the way to town that they talked the whole time and almost forgot to tell Old Man Frank where they were going.

"Where you gals going? Y'all sure is dressed up mighty pretty. Umm umm umm. You Washington girls have always been cute as buttons. But y'all ain't buttons no more!" Old Man Frank tickled himself so that his belly jiggled when he laughed with a closed mouth. Rita often wondered how he did it. He had always been around but didn't start laughing like that until the last few years or so. Rita and her sister laughed at the sight of Old Man Frank's belly jiggling as they always did as they looked at each other like two little giggling girls.

"We are working at that new place in town called the Fox Trot. We will just be saying hello to people and just making them comfortable, not anything serious. Just a little something to make a few dollars, you know."

"Oh yeah," Old Man Frank responded. "I heard of that place. Supposed to be real classy, not like a hole-in-the-wall like some of these other places. You can even call it a juke joint is what I heard."

Rita immediately began to think about what her role would be at the Fox Trot and wanted the pastor's club to be successful. She jumped into action.

"You ought to stop by, Mr. Frank. It's a place for anybody to just come and relax," Rita said naively.

"An old man like me?"

"There is something there for everybody. Quiet music, quiet atmosphere, and quiet times. That's all."

"Well, I may be there directly. Let me get rid of this bushel of corn and I just might do that directly."

"Thanks for the ride, Mr. Frank!" Hattie said as they quickly jumped out of the car.

By this time, Dominique was already at the Fox Trot, inspecting the place for its grand opening. It was almost futuristic because of the modern furniture that dotted the place with luxury and sophistication. The floors were hardwood. The colors that laced the wall were calming. The chairs were cream in color and leather. The complementary colors made the Fox Trot looked as if it was a picture out of a magazine. Colorful flowers were strategically placed to add a splash of boldness, but still soothing to the eye. The ceilings were high. The lines were perfect. It was feng shui before its time. Each piece was strategically placed. The drinking area had the finest glasses. There were highballs and old-fashioneds from whiskey to Collins, all made of the finest crystals. The bar was pure mahogany with a backsplash of glass mirrors to add depth to the area.

In the back, where people wanted a little more privacy, there were sitting areas that were draped by the finest silks to further add to the mystique of the place. There were places designated for napping areas, as they were called, for anyone who needed to lie down for a few minutes privately. This business was beautiful, just as beautiful as the one that was opened across town, about twenty miles away. Dominique couldn't wait for the doors to swing open with patrons. But the fact that they swung open with Rita and Hattie would do, for now.

Rita and Hattie could not believe their eyes at the beauty they were experiencing. They had never seen any place so beautiful and elegant. Rita thought that the Fox Trot was just as beautiful as Dominique.

"Hello, Hattie," Dominique said confidently, like she had met Hattie a dozen times before, but she had never met her not even once.

"Pastor! I am so glad that you asked that I come along with sissy. I am so excited. I have never had a real job before, and I won't let you down."

"This is more than a job," Dominique said. "This will be a way of life. This place will change your lives forever. You stepped over the threshold as girls. But you will depart as women."

That statement was the most profound saying that Hattie had ever heard. She was certainly mesmerized and in a trance just like her sister had been for days.

Dominique continued, as she was looking as beautiful as the day before, "Girls, this is a very important responsibility that you have ahead of you. You are the face of this building. You are me. You have to always remember that. Treat the patrons that are coming in as if they are the most important person in the world. Smile at them. Look intently in their eyes, like they can have you anytime they want. Make them feel like they are at home away from home,

Praise the Lord. You must make them feel as if they want to return here. The better the business does, the better you girls will do."

Dominique told a half-truth, for she knew that no one would prosper from this business but Mr. Sampson, at least for a little while, and herself.

Mr. Sampson, who was standing over against the wall, observing, began to quietly ease over to Dominique and the two vulnerable girls that stood before him.

"Ms. Hattie, you come with me. We have our own business," Mr. Sampson said as he reached for Hattie's hand like a long-lost father. You have your own place to run. The Blue Front is waiting for you."

Rita and Hattie were so excited. They had their own spots to run as if they were their own business. Mr. Sampson and Hattie drove away into the sunset to beat an anticipated rush of eager new patrons to a new establishment for the evening.

"You wait right here, Rita," Dominique said softly as her lips grazed Rita's cheek. As Rita sat, Dominique walked through the Fox Trot one more time to ensure every item was in place. She knew that the feminine prowess of these girls could make or break her. This was also her only way to grow her congregation, as she had specially made napkins that had the name of her church embossed on them. This subtle advertisement would surely get a few repenting souls into the church on Sunday, straight into her pews. Dominique prayed to the Lord as she walked through the place, praying that her businesses would be successful and praying that the girls could pull it off. For if they didn't, the girls would be fools to want to experience the wrath of Dominique that they had not met before. "Amen," she said aloud as she finished her prayer.

The ten o'clock hour was there. The line was wrapped around the building. But by now, Dominique had long disappeared away from the crowd that could associate her with the ungodliness of the world. She could not afford to tarnish her reputation or risk being seen as a hypocrite by living in the world. This would surely ruin her chances at becoming one of the most successful female ministers in the state. In the world. She wasn't even going to spy on either one of the lounges that evening. She was going to leave it to Mr. Sampson to do the running back and forth between the two. By now, Dominique's mind quickly went into the financial aspects of the two businesses. With two thriving businesses on the first day and after all expenses of paying bartenders, the jazz band, and the house girls that Mr. Sampson provided, surely, her portion of the take would be around $15,000, which would be more than enough to start two churches. And then with the offering that the churches would bring in from the patrons at the clubs, that would be enough to open even more establishments across the state.

The night was long. Dominique was on edge, if only she knew what was happening. Dominique had absolutely nothing to worry about. At least with the patronage of the business. If Dominique was a fly on the wall, she would have seen Rita in action. Rita was a wonderful hostess. All the men, both married and single, had a hard time keeping their eyes off her, but especially the single men.

As night falls . . .

"Good evening and welcome. I am so glad you can come. I am Rita, your hostess for the evening. We have several offerings for you tonight. May I suggest that you start by unwinding with a drink, and then Sally here can escort you to the back, if you'd like, to prop your feet and get a load off. Does that sound good to you, sir?" Rita said seductively to a middle-aged man that came in. The middle-aged man was speechless. He was not only mesmerized by the beauty of the hostess, but by the beauty of the nightclub. He wished that she could escort him to the back as well as Sally. It didn't matter; they were both equally beautiful.

"Hello there," the man answered as he lusted after a statue of beauty that he would never have. "I would like a drink to unwind of course, and if you have some soft, comfortable chairs in the back, that would be wonderful. I do have this crick in my neck. It's just awful."

"I am so glad to hear you say that. I love that there is something here that our customers would enjoy doing. It just makes me feel so good and warm inside," Rita replied in an almost-seductive tone, but careful not to come off as too sexy.

"Sally here will be your personal hostess for the evening, sir. She will be able to help you with all of your needs. After your drink, Sally will give you this card. You can choose the amount of time you will need your parts massaged. I suggest an hour. You look like you have been working so hard, yet your big, strong muscles look so tired. All they need is a little rubbing, and I am sure that the tension will just gush right out like a spigot," Rita suggested as she hoped he would spend a lot of time with her. She was starting to learn that time was money.

As night falls . . .

Sally went over to grab the gentleman's arm and escorted him to the bar. Sally was very beautiful, and the middle-aged man would stay attached to her arm all night, if he could. Little did he know yet that anything was possible that evening. Rita was glad that she made an impact on the middle-aged man. This meant that Dominique would be proud of her. This also meant that Rita had another person inside of her that could appear at just the right moment. She was so proud of herself and began to wonder how long the man would be there that evening. Rita kept count of how many patrons came into the nightspot that night. At last count, at least four hundred people came in. Women. Men. Couples. They were all there. And they each had a napkin engraved with Dominique's church on it. Rita knew that thousands of dollars poured into the club that night, just like the liquor poured from the bottles and just like men and women frequented other areas of the club. If Rita didn't know any better, she could have sworn that she recognized some of those girls from the church that were working the rooms for the patrons to relax. But she couldn't be concerned with that. What a flaw in thinking that was. There were dozens of Rita's working that night, some that have passed through the arms of Dominique to get there. But since Rita was instructed only to speak to the patrons that were coming in, she would never know that they too have had private moments with Dominique.

The night went by quickly. Had the morning hours not come in on the rays of the sunshine that were starting to break through the night, Rita would not have realized that the entire night had passed, and she didn't even know it because of the people that came throughout the night. Rita didn't even notice that Mr. Sampson had come through a side door a dozen times, constantly checking on the money that was being spent that evening. The money was coming in so quickly that Mr. Sampson spent every moment counting mounds of money. Mr. Sampson's eyes looked at so much money that evening, even he was surprised at the amount of people who were looking for a little liquor and a little loving care. He was happy with the take that evening, dropped Rita and Hattie off, and then went home. He didn't give a second thought to what Dominique's share would be of the profit of the evening, for he had already formulated a plan that he could be happy with.

Dominique could not wait to meet with Mr. Sampson and receive the thousands he was to give her that day. Had she not been a pastor, she would have gone to get the money herself. But she felt comfortable with Mr. Sampson, and she knew that she could trust him. She was already seated at their meeting spot, the restaurant. No one would question a meal that they would have together. It was only dinner.

"Hello, Dominique, you are as beautiful as ever."

Cut the small talk, she thought to herself. "Mr. Sampson," she replied, "it is so good to see you again. I know the businesses did well that evening based upon my projections. I thought about it thoroughly, and I know that our figures match."

"Well, not exactly," he said slyly. "You are more beautiful than I."

They both chuckled but were eager to get down to business.

"Let's get down to business, shall we?" Mr. Sampson said as Dominique nodded.

"Well, here are two books from last night," Mr. Sampson stated.

Dominique was stunned. The figures had exceeded what she had expected. She had struck gold.

"Now, for the expenses," he added as Dominique put on her poker face,

"there was the bartender, the parking attendant, the lady attendants, the alcohol, the printing fees, the establishment fees, and of course, my fee, which leaves your share for the evening, but from both clubs, $3,000."

Dominique was livid. But even in her anger and her instinct to dispute her take, Dominique said, "Why, Mr. Sampson, I am totally surprised at the amount as I was expecting less. I am so glad that we have joined forces together to make this town happy, my church flourish, and our pockets and purses fatter." Then she rose from the table. "This money will help me start up my next church on the West Coast, along with another business."

"Deal?"

"Deal."

Dominique left the restaurant, knowing that she had to get rid of Mr. Sampson.

As Dominique thought of the night's events, for a moment, she felt as if her dreams of starting her churches were slowly going down the drain. She knew that if she continued with Mr. Sampson, he would derail her dreams forever, and she would never get to where she wanted to be. The idea of him making money off her and stuffing his own pockets made her sick at the stomach by the very thought of it. Dominique knew that she had to act quickly. Money was time, and it was costing her by the minute. Dominique knew that she had to come up with a plan to get rid of the only roadblock to her success. In a flash, she thought how she could get rid of him while keeping her hands clean.

As she devised her plan, she knew that Bennie must come back into the picture. She knew that she could not risk getting her hands dirty. Dominique prepared for bed as the sun was beginning to rise. Once in her bed, she thought for what seemed like hours on how she would get rid of Mr. Sampson. But in reality, the plan was constructed from beginning to end in less than five minutes.

Dominique rose the next morning, rested, refreshed, and knowing that if she were going to get rid of Sampson, it would have to be tonight. She knew that Bennie was only a whisper away, so surely, she could scrounge him up with a moment's notice. But she would have to act quickly. She could not go another night knowing that Mr. Sampson would be collecting the money from the establishments that she knew rightfully belonged to her. This would be the biggest test ever of her commitment to herself.

Getting in touch with Bennie proved to be harder than Dominique thought. She could always contact him, but this time, he was showing himself to be quite elusive. Dominique was worried, knowing that a shift in Bennie's behavior left questions in her mind. Dominique definitely did not want to have anyone around her that she had to wonder if they were completely loyal to her. Many flags were raised in her mind. But if she could just get through this task, then she would figure out what to do with Bennie later.

Dominique waited for what seemed like hours for word that Bennie had gotten her message. She was in such deep thought, she barely heard the knock at the door.

"Ms. Dominique, Mr. Bennie said that the special guest will meet you at the church at 5:00, and your guest should be there by 5:30," the nameless figure said at the door.

Dominique gave a quick nod, got dressed, and sped away to the meeting in the place that had become most familiar and comforting to her: the church.

"Mr. Sampson, I am so glad that you could meet me here," Dominique said as calmly as possible.

"Anything for such a fine business partner," he replied as he stared at Dominique as if she was an exotic dish.

"I am so glad, Mr. Sampson, that our paths have crossed. I would have never gotten my start in business without you, and I simply wanted to show my appreciation to you tonight before we got started," Dominique said as she stared intently into Mr. Sampson's eyes.

"Dominique, you are so beautiful. It is hard to believe that you are a minister and businesswoman all rolled into one. You have to be every man's dream."

Dominique pressed her body even closer to Mr. Sampson, hoping that Bennie would walk in at any second to see their embrace. It was 5:30. Where was Bennie? This plan would have to be timed perfectly in order for Bennie to get the full effect of what was going on in her office.

Just as she was starting to think that the plan wouldn't work, she heard footsteps outside of her door. Dominique prayed that it was Bennie and that he would storm in any minute.

"Oh, Mr. Sampson," Dominique said as loudly as possible, but still in what some would interpret as a sexy voice.

By this time, in an instant, Bennie stormed in and, in his horror, saw Dominique and Mr. Sampson at what he thought was an unsolicited embrace by an imposing figure. In a moment, Bennie saw a blow poke by the fireplace, grabbed it, and struck Mr. Sampson once in the back of the head, rendering him unconscious. He slumped to the ground like a lifeless lump of clay. Dominique was simply glad that Bennie came in on cue and was unmoved by the lifeless body that was in a pile on the floor.

"Oh my, Bennie! You are such a lifesaver! I don't know what I would have done had you not come in. Mr. Sampson would have surely overpowered me, and I would have been a tarnished woman for sure."

"Dominique, I would never let anyone harm you. Never. I am glad that I came in when I did."

"Thank you, Bennie. But I have to get him out of my office before prayer service begins."

"Dominique, don't you worry. I know just the place to put him."

Bennie, although short and stout in stature, dragged Mr. Sampson out to an old, abandoned well in the back of the church. Dominique, with the murder weapon in hand, followed Bennie like he had followed her in many situations before. Bennie, all dressed in one of his best suits, removed the concrete lid of the old well and pushed Mr. Sampson, head first, into the well. Had they checked, they would have noticed that Mr. Sampson was breathing shallowly. But by the time he hit the bottom of the well, he was definitely dead. Before Bennie could rise up from his knees, Dominique swung the blow poke with all her might and struck Bennie on the back of the head. Bennie lay unconscious, with his body halfway in the well. Dominique then got on her knees in her Sunday best and pushed the rest of Bennie's body in the well. There lay two lifeless bodies in a well that had long since stopped providing water for generations of long ago who toiled in the field from sunup to sundown, with the blow poke tossed in the well for good measure. Now the well served a different purpose. The well was now a tomb for two pawns in Dominique's life that were no longer needed. Dominique now had another skill she could add to her resume: murderer.

"Let me see," Dominique said out loud, as if a clone of herself was there with her that very moment. "Good old Clyde Harold. He has the most means and would probably know of a vacant building I could use to get the club up and running." Dominique had the makings of a plan. All she needed was one more contact, and then she would totally be free of any dependency on anyone else. Dominique knew that she had to be careful. She did not want to make any mistakes. Neither did she want Mr. Harold to think that he would be a permanent fixture in her life. One good thing about it though was that Clyde had been a good friend of Mr. Sampson, and she had seen him in passing. And although they had never met personally, she knew that her feminine wiles could get her what she wanted. Dominique also deduced that Clyde had to know that she had been conducting business with Mr. Sampson because they were not only business partners, they were friends. Dominique felt that even though Mr. Sampson and Clyde probably have the same work ethic, she also believed that Clyde would probably be glad that Mr. Sampson was out of the picture, even though he would not realize it for a few more weeks. Dominique knew that this was her final shot at making it on her own.

On the following day, Dominique had finally gotten in contact with good old Clyde. Dominique decided that she wanted to meet at the old distillery back up in the woods for effect. She also felt that the woods would give her more of a demure look and feel, which was in stark contrast to how she normally presented herself to others. The last think that she wanted was to draw the attention of someone she could barely stand to look at, much less kiss if push came to shove. For the first time in her life, Dominique was unaware of just how beautiful she was. She had become so accustomed to transforming herself into a dress-up doll that she didn't even realize that she was even more beautiful without all the bells and whistles that masked what her real intentions were when it came to dealing with people, especially men. Dominique made sure that she walked to the distillery instead of another means of transportation, for she felt as if a little dust and sweat would add to her unattractiveness. However, the sweat beads that were forming on her picture-perfect face made her skin glow across the hot evening sunlight. Anyone who would have seen Dominique at that moment would have no idea of the venomous black widow that she really was.

From afar, Dominique saw Clyde walking across the field, but he had clearly not walked the entire distance from town. His suit was immaculate. His shoes were shined. His jacket fell perfectly, unlike Bennie's. Bennie's jacket draped his round jellylike belly in such a way that caused him to look more disgusting than he actually was. "Well, old Bennie doesn't have that problem now!" she said to herself and giggled as she thought about his deteriorating body at the bottom of the well. His body was probably so decomposed by now that his old skeleton probably appeared to be grinning, especially if his flesh had rotted away from his mouth, exposing nothing but some teeth that were rotting when he was alive.

Dominique had never seen Clyde in this light before. His confidence as he came closer to her made Dominique swoon with lust. She had never been moved by any man before, yet she was the master at making them think otherwise.

"Dominique," Clyde said in a deep baritone voice that masked the problems he was having in his own life.

"Well, Clyde, I didn't expect you so soon. I would have certainly done a better job of drying myself of this sweat that has me soaking wet."

"Oh, I know that sun can be the devil. But if work needs to be done, then I say its best sometimes to do it yourself."

Clyde was foolish to think that Dominique would even think of slaving out in the hot sun. Pulling his strings would be easier than she thought. He wouldn't recognize a ruse if it hit him square between the eyes.

"Yes, Sir Clyde. I try to stay grounded so that I can connect with my church members. I know they work hard, and I want them to see I'm working hard. You can't get anywhere without working hard."

Clyde studied Dominique's words and mannerisms carefully. He knew that a woman's actions spoke volumes even without one word being spoken. That way, Clyde was never ever caught off guard by a woman's feminine wiles.

"Surely, you didn't call me out here to see how well the church's garden was doing, my dear."

Clyde inched closer to Dominique. He knew that the vibe that was bouncing off his hard body would hypnotize Dominique. Clyde had seen it many times before, especially with younger women. Clyde could see himself and Dominique embraced out there in the hot sun, in a hot, passionate kiss. He was just as attracted to her as she was to him. Clyde didn't mind mixing business with pleasure. But he knew how to get back on the business track as soon as possible. Nothing came between Clyde and his money, no matter how fine she was. But if by small chance one would slip in every now and then, it would never be for more than a few minutes.

Clyde had inched within kissing distance of Dominique, and she didn't even realize it. All she knew was that she couldn't move away from an impending embrace. Dominique was startled back to the present by Clyde's deep baritone voice that seemed to radiate off her rapidly breathing body.

"Of course not, Clyde," Dominique said as she quickly stepped back and looked away from Clyde. "I actually have a proposition for you." Dominique quickly slipped into the role of preacher and minister. "You know how dedicated I am to the Lord, and my sole purpose here on earth is to bring souls closer to God."

"I know that, Dominique. Continue, please."

"I am trying to build another church, and you know how difficult that can be, especially in these days and times."

"Oh god, yes."

"And you also know how Mr. Sampson, your partner, has helped me to procure funds for my church."

"You know, I know all about my business partner's dealings."

Dominique continued, "I believe Mr. Sampson has slipped out of town, and I really need to open another business in order to start another church. One more business would give me just what I need in order for me to officially become one of the most successful female ministers in the business, I mean, ministry."

"Dominique," Clyde started, "You know that I am Sampson's partner, and this seems to go behind his back and cut in on his commissions. I don't think I can do it."

"I know exactly what you are saying. I knew a loyal partner would say that, and I respect that. But I can give you something no one has ever given you before," she said as she inched closer and grabbed hold of his handmade silk tie that few men of the day wore.

"Dominique, if I've had one woman I've had . . ."

"Clyde, I'm not talking about that," Dominique said as looked away coyly. "I am willing to offer you 50 percent. It will be you . . . and I in it together, and profits and other sundries that come with the business can be split right down the middle."

They both grinned at her offer and layers of offers. Dominique was still as cunning and conniving as her mother. Dominique expected that one day, she would kill Mr. Sampson, but she had no idea that once she went out to his car to rummage through his things, she would find nineteen large stacks hiding in the car pocket behind some leaves of uncured tobacco. The smell of the tobacco reminded her of some of her childhood days when she would watch other children slaving in the field, suckling tobacco by the heat of the morning sun. Dominique knew that $19,000 could do no good to dead man Mr. Sampson, and putting the money back into her churches by way of another business would just be her ticket and the last deal she would ever have to make with anyone. Dominique saw herself as many things, but she herself never saw herself as a robber. But then again, a perfect opportunity presented itself for her to get her delicate hands on $19,000, so she took it. She knew that she would have a personal conversation with God lately and ask for forgiveness. She prayed that the world didn't come to an end before then. But if it did, she knew that she would still enter through one of the twelve gates because even though the murder, robbery, and other unfortunate events that she evoked on others occurred, she believed that they all happened for a reason, and that was in the end to help her glorify God through her ministry. Unlike those grifters like Skeeter and his crowd, Dominique felt that she wasn't a fraud but a legitimate businesswoman, not some two-bit hustler.

Turning over $19,000 would be easy. If she could just get the business open and get one of the girls that she knew intimately to slip it into the bottom line of her existing businesses pre-Clyde, he would never notice, nor would she have to give him a cut of her serendipitous windfall by way of Clyde's death.

"You know, I can resist a beautiful woman, but I can't resist a beautiful deal," Clyde said as he verbally sealed a deal with Dominique.

Dominique offered him her wrist to kiss. Clyde took her wrist and pulled her delicate frame to him kissed her passionately but quickly.

"I look forward to doing business with you, Dominque."

"Likewise," she said as they both walked away to their respective locations.

Clyde had officially become the face of her last stairway to the level of success that she wanted to achieve. But something strange was beginning to happen. As she saw Clyde walk away, she noticed how he swaggered across the field, careful not to step on the dunes created by that old mule and plow that had just tilled the soft, dusty dirt for next year's crop. Even in the sweltering heat, Clyde knew that the sun and the field was no place for him because that is not where the green that lined his pockets was found. Money for Clyde was made in tucked-away places that were designed to be an escape for the working Joe in the day and the juke jiving swinger that emerged at night. Clyde's wealth was built on the backs of the beautiful women that entertained the gentlemen looking for a little female companionship that was absent of the worn-out appearance of the wives they loved so dearly at home but had transition from being supple, sexual, and supporting, a graying, aging mother that put satisfying her man on the back coals of the old stove.

But he knew Dominique was not that girl. She was beautiful. As he noticed as hard as she tried not to look beautiful standing out there in the field, that only made her more beautiful, desirable, and more importantly, a piece he could have on his arm and have an intimate relationship with, which included giving his heart to her. Clyde had been through many women, and he gave them all no hope or expectation that he would be theirs. As soon as the sun hinted that it was about to peak from around the clouds, he was out of that woman's bed onto the next business venture for the day. Dominique made him feel different. He wanted to feel her. He wanted to feel her breath against his cheek as he gently held her close. Something was telling him that she was the one for him, one that could help him with his business and with is his heart.

"Mr. Clyde." By now, Dominique had pulled out a fan that she could open with the flick of her small wrist to match her small frame.

"Clyde, please."

"Clyde, if it's all the same to you, let's meet tonight at the Carnal Corner. You know the one, where you saw Mr. Sampson and his friend Buford the other night."

Dominique was trying to distance herself from Mr. Sampson's disappearance and death.

"But of course, bring a deposit of, let's say, $5,000, which is my flat fee, I forgot to mention, and then I will give you the preliminary information that I would have found out by then about the Cat's Cradle."

The mention of Mr. Sampson's name made him realize that he hadn't seen his partner in a week or so, and perhaps he should track down Buford to see how much longer Sampson was going to be out of town. It's not that Clyde cared for Sampson, but Sampson had his cut of the $19,000 he knew he was holding. And without that, Sampson was unable to carry on business as usual because of his missing money that Sampson was supposed to hand over the other night. He knew that Sampson normally didn't stay out of town this long for the businesswomen or other responsibilities. And he certainly didn't hold on to his money this long. And Sampson would do anything to anyone that got in the way of his money, even if it was his own money.

Dominique didn't know that Clyde's situation was dire. Without his cut of the $19,000, his own personal business ventures were on hold, which offered the prime opportunity for others to saturate the business, especially using the contacts that had taken him so long to create. Clyde just couldn't see that happening and was willing to do anything to remain at the front of the race. He was going to give Sampson another week to get back in town, but after that, Clyde decided that he would eliminate Sampson himself, if he found him, just for the simple fact that he caused him to worry about his money, or he would eliminate anyone else that he deemed was responsible for his setback.

Dominique was excited about getting over this last hurdle, but she was even more excited about getting to know Clyde a little better and tapping into his business sense to see how she can continue to become and stay successful. On second thought, she better not be so quick to get rid of him after all. She was excited about the meeting at the Cat's Cradle tomorrow evening because she knew that this meeting would put her one step closer to opening another church and another business. She wanted so bad to be the first nationwide pastor. She wanted everyone to know her name. She wanted man, woman, saint sinner, Jew, and Gentile to always be pulling on her for her ministry, her singing, or her business sense. This would help her prove that she was worthy to hang in there with the best of them, especially the males. She wasn't worried about female pastors because neither were they businesswomen, nor were they beautiful. They would always be some old female minister that would get up in the pulpit, hoot and holler for a minute, all decked out in some form of a white suit, white stockings, and white shoes, and there they would remain for the rest of the lives: nowhere. Clyde was her ticket. He would be the last piece of the puzzle, only if she could reel him in.

The next day, even Clyde waited in anticipation of meeting Dominique at the Cat's Cradle that evening. She knew she had to be careful though with that $19,000. One whisper of its origins, and she could be hanging from a tree somewhere at the hands of her own kind. Men didn't play with their money or their women, so she knew she had to be extremely careful of what she said and what she did around Clyde. She knew at some point, old Sampson's name would come up. But it couldn't come up in the context of where Clyde could be with money he may had had on him, for Clyde was known to carry some money around with him, and everyone knew it but never bothered him about it.

Clyde had shown up at the Cat's Cradle because he loved to see the young beautiful female workers come in and maybe even sample the goods before they offered their services. But even with his sampling for the evening, he still could not get the beautiful Dominique off his mind. Just as he was coming out of the back of the massage room with a beautiful woman, Dominique appeared, dressed in her Sunday best, ready to save any souls that needed a healing that night. She did not want to let on that she was there to patron the Cradle. But everyone knew Dominique, and she was not there to have a good secular time by any means. Strangely, Dominique was aroused in many ways by seeing Clyde emerge from the back with such a beautiful woman. The woman was so beautiful that Dominique made a mental note to meet with her sometime on Sunday because she was a member she recognized from church. Her full supple lips made Dominique's own lips water at the thought of planting a peck on her youthful pucker. Clyde and this girl were beautiful together. Perhaps she and Clyde could meet with the beautiful girl privately, and who knows where that meeting would take them.

"Minister Dominique! There you are. Over here!" Clyde exclaimed as he motioned with his size 12 finger for her to meet him and the Cradle beauty that was on his arm.

"Minister Dominique, I know you are out of your element, and I see why you are here. This is Ada, and she provides a wonderful service here to the patrons."

"Pleased to meet you," Dominique replied as she reached out for Ada's soft, lineless hand. Dominique could imagine herself caressing Ada's hand as she offered counseling or some other service to her in her office.

"Run along, Ada, I will see you some other time, perhaps," Clyde said.

The word "perhaps" alone just reiterated to Dominique that Clyde didn't need a beautiful woman, nor was it a challenge for him to get one, for any purpose, if he so chose. That was another sign of confidence that she admired in Clyde.

"Dominique, I am so glad you could make it. Have you cracked that Bible tonight?"

"I read my Bible daily, and it helps to connect with lost souls."

"I am glad we had the chance to connect. You are so beautiful and smart. I can see us to continue to be in business together, Dominique. It doesn't have to end here. We can rule the world."

"Clyde, I don't like crowds, especially men who goes around thinking that can manipulate any man or woman that crosses their path. I'm not that woman."

"And I am not that man. Your rouse in the field didn't fool me. I knew what you wanted before I got there. I saw how you tried to downplay yourself for me. We don't have time for that, my dear. You need me, and I need you, and we both need more money. We can partner for the sake of the money, and we can both get what we want."

"Clyde, that is such an excellent idea. I could not have said the words better myself. I just want you to be sure that–"

"Listen here, Dominique. I am a man. I am the man," Clyde said sharply, yet delicately to not arouse suspicion of his true character to Dominique. "If this is going to work, then you must allow me to work these connections and allow me to get both of us where we need to go. You only need me for a season just like I only need you for a season. But if you think that you are going to make a wimp out of me like Bennie and the others, then you have found the wrong partner."

"Clyde, I would never jeopardize me getting to where I need to go. But don't push me. I make my own way. You can be the man, but you certainly won't be the boss of me. I–"

Clyde interrupted Dominique with a passionate kiss, and she could not pull away. She was not even concerned that someone could walk by any second and see them embrace in a fit of passion that blackened out the rest of the club. With what seemed like seconds, that kiss seemed like an eternity for Dominique. While Dominique was so engrossed by the trap of Clyde's strong embrace, Clyde, the slickster-businessman that he was, had his eyes wide open scanning the room for potential hazards that could ruin Dominique. He didn't want that. He knew that her demise with a ruined reputation would hamper his abilities to get his hands on this much-needed loot that this club was bound to rake in. As he predicted when she was about to open her eyes, he quickly closed his to match the emotional involvement that she was emitting at the time.

For the first time in a long time, Dominique felt something that she had never felt before: love. She was in love with Clyde's boldness and sense of self, a stark contrast from simpleminded Bennie and self-conscious Skeeter and his inadequate man parts. Clyde's manliness alone was enough for her to feel what true love was, especially from someone who wanted the same thing in life that she did, and that was money and power. But the more Dominique thought about love, she began to notice that love occupied more of her mind than money did. This was not like her. Nothing came between Dominique and the frequent *ménage à trois* she often had with her love of becoming the most powerful female pastor, male or female, and being able to afford what life had to offer to make her more than comfortable in her endeavors. This battle that Dominique began to have with herself went against everything that she believed in, yet she allowed love to seep in at an attempt of removing her love of the other two entities in her life.

Dominique found herself often fantasizing about being in the grips of Clyde, for when he held her, he also held her heart. She had never felt this way before, nor had she allowed herself to feel this way. She was a one-man show with no room for distractions. But on the other hand, Dominique began to realize that perhaps she and Clyde could be a true team. They both seemed to have the same interest, and he seemed to be straightforward and to the point in all the conversations that they had had previously. He was strong, both mentally and physically. He wanted to take life by the horns. She could sense that he was a good lover. All these things had intrigued Dominique, and they left her yearning to become more connected with her business partner, Clyde. Dominique felt whole, and she felt as if God was granting her everything that she wanted.

Dominique continued to be lost in her thoughts of love with Clyde. The thought of loving Clyde suddenly flooded her entire existence. What puzzled even herself was that she had known Clyde for just a short period of time. No one event had ever held her as captive as the undeniable love she had felt for Clyde whom she felt was her true soul mate. Dominique had counseled many on the ups and downs of love, and she had always told herself that she would never fall into that trap. Yet here she was, on the opposite side of the aisle, trapped in the throes of love that she had no desire to overcome. Dominque could hardly sleep because of her eagerness and longing to be in the arms of Clyde once again. She knew that she would have another chance to see him as soon as the sun went down tomorrow evening.

Clyde was smitten with the presence of Dominique. He knew that she was a woman that he probably could marry, but he also knew that playing around with fire, especially one as hot as Dominique, could derail his plans forever. Any plan. Clyde was accustomed to visiting women that could be considered a 6 or a 7 on a scale of 1 to 10, but Dominique was a flat-out 10. Tens could be dangerous. They were beautiful, smart, ambitious, and sexy, and most of them were black widows. One sting from a black widow and a man's life could be ruined forever. The money would be gone along with the dignity. Clyde was not willing to risk that. But he wanted Dominique. She was made especially for him. Clyde had never fantasized about a woman before, but he fantasized about Dominique. He fantasized about her submitting her body and mind to him. He wanted to caress every inch of her delicate body, from her long curly locks, her voluptuous body, her perfectly aligned frame, all the way to the tip of her feet devoid of any corns and calluses. He knew the taste of her body was sweet. He knew that the moisture of her body would drip like honey from his lips. He knew that she would be receptive to him and to his urges. Clyde had been around enough women to know who wanted him for physical or financial purposes and who loved him. Dominique loved him, and he knew it. He wanted to reciprocate by offering his heart to her. But Clyde was certain that his money and his businesses would not be compromised for his love of Dominique. He suddenly snapped out of his self-imposed trance, knowing that he would have Dominique on his terms. Unlike Dominique, one thing such as love did not occupy his mind at one time. Clyde was also wondering what had happened to his partner Bennie. He was losing money by the day.

The sun came up the morning, making its usual appearance on a world that had been blanked with darkness for the past few hours. Many acts had been committed, and many secrets have been created in such a short period of time. The sunlight made it appear like those things didn't even happen. The world was reset on rewind, and new memories and dreams would be created once again.

As night falls . . .

Dominique was dressed, and she was eager to collect her earnings from the clubs for the previous night. Dominique was making money hand over fist. She was inching closer and closer to become the most successful female minister of all time. She loved making the rounds of collecting her money. It made her feel powerful. It made her feel that she was on this earth to do what she was supposed to do and to live the life she was supposed to live. She loved her life, and she loved Clyde. She knew when she saw him tonight, she should be more discreet. She could not risk anyone finding out that she had a dual life. That could mean disaster for her ministry, and it would close any doors to her ever making the kind of money she was making from the clubs. Hopefully, she was to get a glimpse of him sometime after hours. Right then, there was a knock at the door that startled Dominique from her daydream.

Dominique answered the door, completely covered in a matching silk housecoat and matching mules with the fur on the toe.

"Yes?" she said as she peeped around the door.

"Here is a message for you. Have a good evening." The young man quickly left her door without any further information.

Dominique opened the note slowly and prayed to the Lord that it was from Clyde.

The note read, "Meet me tonight at 3:00 a.m. I must see you. The address is below. And it is safe."

Dominique's heart fluttered with anticipation. She could not wait to see Clyde tonight.

As Dominique waited for the day to slowly go by, she immersed herself with her biblical readings, Bible study, and counseling. Her heat was completely into it. One thing she could do was to compartmentalize and to keep separate her commitment to God and her desires for worldly pleasures. She knew that God would continue to bless her because of her commitment and faithfulness to the ministry and to the work of the Lord. Dominique loved what she did. And she loved money just as much. She knew just as soon as the evening service was over, that she was going to rush over to the cabin where Clyde would be waiting. She would not have to get dressed, for under her ministerial robe was her seductress attire for the evening. She was going to make sure that Clyde saw her in her full beauty. She was so glad when the last member left so that she could make her way to the cabin that was at least an hour and a half away. She could tell that Clyde was committed to being discreet. It was another quality that she loved about him.

Dominique daydreamed all the way to the cabin. She could not believe that she was going to finally be with a man that she had fallen in love with so quickly. She could anticipate the scent of his body and the embrace of his safe arms. As she walked into the cabin, she saw how beautiful it was. There was an evening robe left for her to slip into. The fireplace was on, and there was some mellow jazz playing on the recorder in the back. The bed was covered with rose petals with a note that read, "Just for a queen." Dominique threw herself on the bed, almost in a childlike manner. Bennie would turn over in his death state if he saw this side of her. Dominique was wondering why she couldn't get Bennie off her mind. He was on her mind just as much as Clyde was. Perhaps she intrinsically felt that what was done in the dark would surely come out in the light.

Dominique came back to herself once again. She was about to burst with anticipation of what Clyde had in store for her. Her heart was beating rapidly, and her mind was racing as if it were on the Kentucky Derby. Dominique knew that the rose petals were a good sign. What an outward sign of love they were. The way that the petals were scattered over the bed was symbolic to her that Clyde's love would stretch far and near. The deep color of the petals were the color of cold blood, cold blood that ran deep in the veins of many. Life. The start of a new one with Clyde, she dreamed.

Dominique didn't even notice that Clyde had eased in the door, admiring the true beauty before him. Dominique looked like a piece of clay that had never been molded by the hands of any man. She looked pure as she sat arrested by her thoughts. Clyde wanted her, and he wanted her badly. He had played this moment out in his mind like he did with many women, but Dominique was something special, and he knew in his heart that she belonged to him.

"Dominique."

As night falls . . .

There were no other words that were uttered that night by neither Clyde nor Dominique. The rhythm of their breathing and the rhythm of their hearts were the only signs of human occupancy of that love villa. The sun ushered in another day, and Clyde and Dominique lay there in each other's arms, basking in the afterglow of a love-filled passionate night.

"Marry me."

Dominique was so taken by Clyde's words that she could not even respond. She had anticipated those words jumping off his lips for weeks. She felt like she was in a trance, hypnotized by the man that had penetrated her being on so many levels.

Marriage was a thought that had never crossed Dominique's mind. She never saw marriage as anything that was palatable, but rather a burdensome condition of internal and external imprisonment. She had seen what marriage had done to young hopeful women dreaming of riding off into the sunset on a white horse and carriage, and instead, finding a buster who is buried in layers of Prince Charming's cape that came off as soon as the lights went off. But she saw Clyde differently. She experienced the many layers that he had and how much of herself that she saw in him. How much of a more perfect fit was there. There was none. Dominique was ready to walk down the aisle. She was ready to solidify this union. She was ready to add more to her net worth, and what better way to do it than with a man that she loved.

"And we must do it quickly," Clyde added. "I don't believe in waiting around, nor do I particularly care if we didn't advertise it to the world. If people found out, then fine with me. I won't deny it, but I'm not one to broadcast my business. Meet me at Johnny's Jivin' Juke Joint tomorrow night at 6:00 p.m. I have a 'marriage certificate man' who will hook it right up." Clyde had a "man" or "woman" for everything. He never had to look far for whatever service he needed. So there would be no fanfare, no doves, no bridesmaids (not that Dominique had a cache of women to choose from). But a union of two lovers joining as one in front of the Lord would suffice.

The day of the ceremony, Dominique could not believe what was happening. She could not believe that she was going to have the life she wanted and the man she desired. Now her life was going to be complete. She was going to have them all. Now she really would. Her life was now going to be complete, and she didn't even know it was empty until she met Clyde. Clyde showed up at Johnny's in a custom-made suit. This one, however, was special. It was especially made by one of those West Coast tailors, a style that had never been produced before and would never be produced again. Clyde wore all white, symbolic of the pure feelings that he had for Dominique. Dominique, in turn, had on a simple white dress, one that would not easily be recognized as a wedding dress, but beautiful just the same. Dominique was even more beautiful than anyone had ever seen before. The glow that was emitting from her radiant skin accentuated the beauty that she possessed. Clyde's man was already there.

"Sign here, and that will be $100 for convenience, of course," he said. Dominique signed as tears stained the certificate, and Clyde's followed. And with that, the man was gone. Now Dominique and Clyde had become Mr. and Mrs. Clyde Smith.

"Dominique, this is going to be the start of our life as one. We will dominate the world of ministry and clubs. It won't start here. We can make millions. We will be some rich colored folks around here. You can continue building your ministry, and I will continue to build the businesses until I decide that it is time for both of us to get out."

"Clyde, I will. I will follow your lead. I will hold up my end of this deal. I love you, and I know that both of us can take this world by storm."

"Dominique, this marriage is unconditional. You must not have any secrets from me, but you must not question some of the things I decide regarding business. I know these jokers, so I can better deal with them. As soon as you start dealing with them, these slimy boys will want more from you, and I am not going to risk that. If that happens, you must tell me everything. Our relationship will be built on trust and trust alone. Just be open with me and I will always take care of your needs, no matter what they are," Clyde concluded.

Dominique looked at Clyde coyly, wondering if he knew about some of her trysts that occurred between the testimonies and the tears in the office. She sensed he knew, but she dared not ask.

"Of course there will be no secrets. I will tell you everything."

"Very well, darling, we must rest. For tomorrow, we have business to conduct."

Dominique's honeymoon was all she could have hoped for. Clyde and Dominique talked all night about their lives, but especially about their ambition. Dominique was amazed at Clyde's brazen honesty. He opened up about his wealth, his goals, his dreams, and his crimes, crimes that he had never spoken of before tonight. Dominique was intrigued. She was not intrigued about the tales, but about his honesty. She was ready to give herself to him again. Perhaps this was time for her to rid herself of that pesky Bennie that kept occupying her mind. Perhaps his murder was trying to escape her conscience, along with Mr. Sampson's.

"Clyde, I love you so much, I don't want to go into our marriage any further with any secrets."

"Speak, my love," Clyde retorted.

"Clyde, I have always wanted to be a successful woman. I have wanted to be in charge of my own life, make my own money, and make my own decisions. Many women that I grew up admiring did not have these qualities. They were not as fearless as I am. I go for what I want. And I didn't allow anyone or anything to get in my way," she continued.

"Continue, my dear."

"Mr. Sampson was cheating me out of thousands of dollars a night. He was really destroying me. So I had to do something."

"What did you do, darling?"

As night falls . . .

"One night, he and I were meeting at the church and having a good old time, hoping he was there to make things right. Yes, we did kiss, but I felt that he was becoming more aggressive in his kiss," Dominique embellished. "So as I was engrossed in his strong arms, Bennie came in, assessed the scene, and hit him with a blow poke that killed him instantaneously. I was in utter shock!"

"My Lord, have mercy!" Clyde exclaimed. "Then what happened, love?"

"He was dead for sure. Bennie checked. So we got him to this old well and slid him in gently to dispose of him humanely. Then I became worried about Bennie and his willingness to keep quiet. His emotions blew like the wind. I couldn't trust him, and he became a liability. So I had no choice but to knock him off and to slide him in the well along with Mr. Sampson."

Normally, Dominique would have cried in genuine tears, but there was no need to since she wanted to be an honest woman with Clyde.

"Oh, baby, don't worry about it. You did what was necessary to survive. You did what was necessary to stay on top. Let's get some rest, and tomorrow is a new day," he said softly with a kiss to her forehead. "I am going out of town on business, but I want you to discretely ease in the club on Madirose Street to pick up the money that will be wrapped in a white cellophane. Put it in the sacks that will be there and get out as soon as you can. I want my woman and her money to be warm and tucked in by the time I get home."

Dominique was excited. She could hardly wait to get her hands on the money that was hers.

Dominique slept all day, anticipating her take for the evening. She stood to make $30,000 and could hardly wait to get her hands on them. She was well disguised for the evening. Her attire was fitting for slipping in and slipping out to pick up a load of loot. She figured she wear all black, with her hair in a wispy updo. If there were any congregants there, and she was sure that there would be, they would not recognize her because normally, she wore her hair down. Dominique had an ageless beauty, and she looked ten years younger with her hair up. But for once in her life, she didn't know it. She was focused on the cash that awaited her.

Dominique sauntered into the club to the back where the safe was. A big burley gentleman recognized her, much to her surprise, and without looking at her, pointed in the direction of the safe. And there it was. The first real fruits of her labor. Her money, her love. She grabbed the cellophane-wrapped goods and proceeded to the back door. As she moved briskly to her car to get out of the cold, crisp air, she noticed a car in the distance and felt that she must be more careful, because she saw no driver.

"Someone must have broken down," she said out loud.

As Dominique was getting in her car, she heard a loud, shrill voice that exclaimed, "Stop! Put your hands up!"

Dominique kept walking, unaware that the voice was directed toward her.

"Lady, stop! Or I will shoot!"

Dominique turned around slowly to see what the commotion was. Much to her surprise, there were officers who had guns trained on her.

"Why, Officers, there must be . . ."

"Stop and drop that package!"

Dominique realized that this was real, and they were talking to *her*. Before she knew it, one of the officers grabbed the package and quickly began to open it.

"Yep, they were right. This lady must be Lady Heroin."

"Officer, you must be mistaken. That is just some money that I had at the club there that belongs to my church. Please look carefully."

Before Dominique knew it, she was cuffed and placed in the back of the squad car. She wasn't worried. She knew Clyde would work it out for her.

Dominique, even in a crisis, remained collected during this arrest.

"Officers, I must make a phone call as soon as we get to the office. My husband will sort this all out for me," she said confidently.

"Yes, they all do, madam, and I am sure he will."

The officer arrived at the station with Dominique, who looked as stunning as ever. He immediately escorted her to the telephone so that she could place a call and left her alone for privacy.

Dominique was thrilled to get a line out to Clyde.

"Clyde, I am in a little tight. Please come meet me at the police station because there has been some kind of misunderstanding," she said.

"Of course I will be there. I'll be there right away, Dominique."

Clyde was at the station within minutes.

"Dominique Smith, please."

"Right this way, sir."

The officer escorted Clyde to Dominique's cell. She was so excited to see him that she probably saw him before he realized she was actually there.

"Darling!" For the first time in a long time, Dominique broke down in tears. She wasn't afraid but relieved that someone who loved her so much would come to her rescue.

"Darling, I was mistakenly given heroin instead of the money. You know these officers. Please straighten it out for me so that we can get out of here."

"Dominique," Clyde started, "I do know these officers, just like I knew my brother."

"Your brother? Who, my love?"

"You would know him by the name of Sampson, but I called him Sammy." And with that, he walked away.

Dominique never felt so alone in her life. She was in jail. Her love had abandoned her, and her ministry was starting to become a faint dream. Dominique fell on her knees and began to pray and sing verses 1 and 2 from the hymn "Amazing Grace." She had never felt so low in her life. She had no one to call, and for once in her life, she could not fix her problem. Only God could fix her problem and help her out of this mess. Dominique felt like Paul and Silas. She sang hymns and prayed all night that the Lord would give her strength to make it through this crisis. She didn't even realize that the sun was coming up because she had no access to windows, no way for God's light to shine through the gloomy walls of the jail.

"Mrs. Smith," a strange voice said.

"Mrs. Smith?" he repeated.

"Yes," she said softly.

"I am your attorney. I'm here to assist you with your case. Can you tell me what happened?"

"Yes, I can," she started. "I strayed from the safety of his arms and didn't even know it. I strayed from the safety of his arms. That is what has landed me here."

"Mrs. Washington, this is very, very serious. That was a large amount of heroin you were faced with. And I am afraid that if you do not take a plea offer of two years, you could be facing twenty. And you won't be a pretty young thing in twenty years, so you best get out in two . . ."

"Son, the prison I am already in is far worse than the physical bars that are before me."

"You have just a few days, ma'am. Court is in two weeks."

"I'll do two years. It is the prison I deserve for the sins I have committed."

Waiting for a trial for three years can have a strange effect on a woman. Dominique saw the world differently. She saw that there was much more to life than the tangible things. There was also love, and there was also the Lord, and His blessings are what she desired.

In the total five years that Dominique served behind bars, she saved more souls than she did the many years she was in the ministry. She had even heard that Clyde had a new twenty-two-year-old wife on his arms and that he was happy. That did not stop Dominique from loving Clyde; she still loved him, and in her heart, she forgave him. She knew that when she would be released tomorrow, she would go to see him and tell him that there were no hard feelings, and she would move on.

Freedom felt good to Dominique. She hadn't experienced it in a long time, neither physically nor spiritually. Dominique was as beautiful as ever, but her newfound love of the Lord made her more beautiful than any imported makeup she wore daily. She knew that her first stop would be over to Clyde's to make amends and to let him know that she was truly sorry for her actions. But as she walked in to the sunset, she saw a house that was ablaze, and it was Clyde's! Dominique thought about the jail that she had been in for five years and felt that perhaps it would be appropriate for Clyde to suffer in a smoky, smoldering jail, a far worse fate than what she just experienced. But Dominique immediately ran up the stairs where she hoped Clyde would not be, but there he was, gasping for air and unable to move because of a heavy desk that had fallen on his leg and burned it. With all the strength that she could muster, she pulled a half-conscious Clyde down the stairs and out the front door. Meanwhile, Faith Rae, his wife, sped off as rapidly as possible.

"Clyde, I love you, and I am so sorry. Please forgive me."

"Dominique, I forgive you, and forever I will be indebted to you."

Clyde could not speak after this point since more than 80 percent of his body had been burned. Dominique could not leave him in that state. She had to take care of him, and that was what she vowed to do, if he made it. His recovery would be long and hard, but she would not leave him. She was going to stay by his side, no matter what.

Years had passed, and time moved slowly. The businesses had taken a hit, and people were not coming to church like they used to. Dominique had to work day in and day out to put food on the table. It was arduous. She was starting to feel old, and strangely, beauty was not that high on the priority list anymore; survival was. But she looked as beautiful as she could because she still believed herself to be a classy lady. Her beauty was just hidden momentarily by the trials of life.

As Dominique was leaving work one day, from Ms. Neva's to be more precise, she ran into Mr. Tibbedoau, a familiar face, but an unfamiliar name.

"Ms. Smith! You look great. I haven't seen you in a long time."

"Pleased to see you, but I must get home to Clyde."

"Wait a minute. I know you. You ran the after-hours joints and was the famous minister. I have been looking for you for a while now. I was saddened to hear about the misfortune of great loss you experienced, but one thing I know, there were none as smart as you in this racket." He continued, "There is no way you'll get anywhere just cleaning houses. Your husband is sick and needs a lot of help I am sure. I could help you get back on your feet. You could move out of the projects, hire a nurse for your husband, and you'll be greater this time than you were before! Think about it."

Dominique said, "Well, things are nothing like they used to be for sure, and I'm not going to pretend. I am tired of not making ends meet, and I don't have any money to buy my husband medicine. I feel sorta like I'm wasting away with no hope in sight. I am preaching some and working with the CLFC, the Christian Ladies for Christ, where I do receive quite a bit of joy. It's peaceful, rewarding, and it feels so good to know you're doing a work that pleases God. I have never felt this way before."

"But," said Mr. Tibbedaux, "I am prepared right now, this very moment, to bring you into my organization where you will be just under my authority. You can still do your church and God stuff, and right now, I'm holding this briefcase from my car, and I'm willing to give it to you if we have a deal."

Dominique said, "What's in it?"

Mr. Tibbedaux opened the briefcase, and it was full of hundred-dollar bills. He said, "I want you to have this as a bonus just for saying yes to my proposition."

Dominique replied, "How much money is in the case?"

Mr. Tibbedaux answered, "One million dollars, and I want you to have it."

Dominique, looking perplexed, said, "Wow! That's a lot of money, and it could exorcise quite a few financial demons I'm dealing with and give assistance to my husband and the fellowship, not to mention elevate my lifestyle."

Mr. Tibbedaux replied, "The money, the cars, the homes, all you want will be at your command. Just join us, Dominique."

Dominique knew the money came from a shady and illegal activity, but she said, "Dirty money baptized in the holy water of good is redeemed." So Mr. Tibbedaux placed the briefcase on the ground in front of her, and she extended her arms to embrace Mr. Tibbedaux. Mr. Tibbedaux enthusiastically rushed to Dominique's extended arms. She hugged him very tightly and whispered in his ear, "I'll get back with you." Then she simply pivoted and walked away.

Two days after Dominique, with all her strength, walked away from the million-dollar offer, a new clarity emerged in her consciousness. Her eyes opened, and she saw doctors and nurses, as well as cords connected to her body and breathing machines. The sounds from the machines seemed to get louder and louder. A great excitement began to fill the room, and Dominique, slowly easing into a state of consciousness, smiled with an expression of bewilderment on her face. By now, she was seemingly quite dazed at the sight and scene she was now experiencing; and amid this unexplained moment, she saw her mother, Louise, her sister Lorraine, and her pastor all crying uncontrollably at seeing her eyes opened. Second by second, she was more and more realizing the actuality of the present moment. And with her arms extended and tears slowly rolling down her once totally bewildered face, she then understood that although she had traveled thousands of miles seemingly just moments ago, she now came to recognize she had not gone any farther than the local hospital for Negroes.

She had been in a deep state of unconsciousness; a coma was the medical term. And though this story of murder, robbery, sexual perversion, and an unquenchable thirst for power and money had been told in great detail for all those around her bedside, and she talked almost nonstop for days on end, it was only a dream, a dream that stemmed from the obsession of poverty and her insatiable desire to be emancipated from it. The characters revealed in her dream were all conceived and constructed from a fertile imagination brought on by the trauma of her socially impoverished life. She had traumatically dealt with a condition called MPD, or multiple personality disorder, a condition that stems from what is real and inserting fiction in place of what is factual. With emotional passion, she embraced her mother, sister, and pastor and loudly exclaimed her plans for her future, which were to go on and finish college and continue to study so she could be a doctor of psychology. She wanted to dedicate her life to assisting other young people who might one day suffer from a similar condition. She came to understand this was a coma of clarity that was necessary for her to understand God's purpose for her life.

From that day, she immersed herself in study and received her PhD and lived an exemplary life of spirituality and educational excellence. She educated young black women on the importance of "realizing their worth and never compromising the greatness that God has created in them."

----------END----------

CPSIA information can be obtained
at www.ICGtesting.com
Printed in the USA
LVHW100052021022
729724LV00039B/309